NEMEZIA
AND THE
Wooden Sword

NEMEZIA
AND THE
Wooden Sword

M. C. OLIVEIRA

authorHOUSE®

AuthorHouse™
1663 Liberty Drive
Bloomington, IN 47403
www.authorhouse.com
Phone: 1-800-839-8640

Published by AuthorHouse 08/07/2012

ISBN: 978-1-4772-3723-6 (sc)
ISBN: 978-1-4772-3722-9 (e)

Library of Congress Control Number: 2012912051

Over the mountains of Greenland, there is a whole other world where we all have been at some point in our lives. It is a place we do not talk about or mention, not even to our closest friends. It is a magnificent place, yet it's amazing how we forget about it so quickly, even though it is with us throughout our lives.

Sometimes, a smell of a rose will bring us back to a romantic evening. The smell of apple pie takes us back to Grandma's kitchen. A butterfly flies around us and gives us a sense of how precious life is. Yet we do not remember the most exciting, breathtaking experience of our lives.

Chapter 1

It was almost midnight on this summer evening on Chestnut Street. Miss Jennings was sitting at her white cherrywood vanity in her bedroom, facing a small mirror. With only the moonlight shining through the bedroom blinds, she could barely see herself as she set black curlers in her short, red hair. Her furry white cat, Snowball, lay on the floor near her feet, patiently waiting for her to get into bed so he could climb into the bottom of the sheets. But Miss Jennings was not in a hurry to get into bed that night; she had been waiting for this night for twenty-eight days.

She waited patiently for the dark oak grandfather clock at the end of the hallway to chime midnight. Every few minutes, she would put on her oversized pink-framed eyeglasses to take a quick glance at the clock. Her glasses covered practically half of her face.

"Five more minutes 'til midnight, Snowball," she said excitedly as she rubbed her hands together. She stood up and pulled her green silk nightgown away from her waist, where it was stuck between the rolls of fat. She slowly tiptoed to the window at the right of her bed and separated the blinds with the tips of her fingers, just enough to peek at Mr. Spindle's house. She could see his front porch perfectly from where she was standing.

"He's not there yet, Snowball," she whispered. "We must be patient. I know he'll be home soon."

Mr. Spindle had lived directly across the street from Miss Jennings, at 100 Chestnut Street, for about six months. Miss Jennings was certain that ever since Mr. Spindle moved into the neighborhood, things had not been the same. Mysterious things had happened, and Miss Jennings was determined to get to the bottom of it. She'd been watching him very closely; in fact, she suspected he lived in an empty house, as she'd seen him bring in only a small antique suitcase.

Mr. Spindle's little white cottage was situated in the middle of a small yard, surrounded by a white picket fence. The cottage had black shutters and a porch that wrapped all the way around the perimeter. The beautiful pink and sky-blue roses that grew around his porch gave out a calming scent throughout the neighborhood. Just outside his front door were a small black wicker table and a rocking chair, where he often would drink coffee, smoke cigars, and read the newspaper. Mr. Spindle was tall, thin, and bald, with a thick gray mustache that hung to the middle of his chest. He always dressed in blue overalls with a white T-shirt and black boots. Mr. Spindle walked around with an odd cane that resembled an old tree branch—he would not go anywhere without it. Unlike his neighbor Miss Jennings, Mr. Spindle was a quiet man who minded his own business.

Miss Jennings had noticed that at night, during a full moon, Mr. Spindle looked as if he was going somewhere special. He would wear a black suit with a white button-down shirt and a strange tie with different colored buttons on it. His black dress shoes were so shiny, he could see his reflection in them.

"He looks so silly with that stupid tie!" Miss Jennings would exclaim to her neighbors. Most people thought she had the hots for Mr. Spindle, since she watched his every move.

On this night, Miss Jennings expected nothing different. As her fingers shook nervously in between the blinds, she heard the clock chime midnight. Miss Jennings watched Mr. Spindle's house for several minutes and then noticed him step out onto his front porch. "There he is, Snowball," she whispered with excitement. He had a cigar in one hand and the crooked cane in the other, just as expected. She watched as he sat in his rocking chair, staring at the moon with a smile, seeming to enjoy the cool breeze blowing through his mustache. Miss Jennings looked up at the moon herself to see what he was smiling at, but she didn't see anything except an immense, bright moon. Moments later, however, the leaves on the maple tree in his front yard began changing color—blue, then back to green, and then purple, red, white, and yellow! She then glanced at Mr. Spindle rocking very calmly back and forth in his wicker chair as if nothing unusual was occurring. At first, she thought she was imagining things, so Miss Jennings reached over to grab her glasses from her nightstand. As she slowly separated the blinds once more, she saw that the leaves were brighter than they had been just moments ago.

"I knew it! I knew he was up to something," she whispered to Snowball. Suddenly, the leaves began falling off the tree and, for a few moments, glided around Mr. Spindle's yard. They then began to flap up and down like birds. The leaves set off into the air and flew down the street toward Bella's house. Bella was one of Miss Jennings neighbors. Miss Jennings watched as the leaves surrounded Bella's rooftop. She was so excited that her fingers slipped off the blinds and made a loud clunking noise. She quickly stepped away from the window and waited a few minutes before peeking through again. She didn't want Mr. Spindle to see her spying on him. Holding her nightgown up away from her feet, Miss Jennings peeked once more. To her surprise, Mr. Spindle was no longer on the porch and the leaves had returned to the tree and were green again as if nothing had ever happened.

"Bella isn't going to believe this!" Miss Jennings muttered to herself. She climbed into bed, set her alarm clock for 6:00 a.m., and tried to get some sleep, but she tossed and turned all night—she couldn't keep her mind off the colorful flying leaves. Miss Jennings was still awake when she heard her grandfather clock chime four times—4:00 a.m. Lying in bed, staring at the ceiling, she suddenly had an idea. She kicked her white cotton blanket off of her legs so fast that Snowball went flying onto the floor.

Miss Jennings got up and put on her pink chenille robe and wiggled her pudgy toes into her fluffy pink slippers. She held her finger in the air as she looked at her cat and said softly, "Snowball, I'll be right back." Miss Jennings grabbed her glasses off of the nightstand and tiptoed down the hallway toward the staircase. Snowball stood at the top, watching her hold onto the banister as she carefully walked down the stairs. She reached for the black flashlight in the top drawer of the hutch. With her hand on the doorknob, Miss Jennings slowly opened the door and stepped outside. It was so quiet, all that was heard was the squeaking of the door hinges and the crickets in the bushes. Holding up her robe above her ankles, she tiptoed over the debris in her front yard as she approached the broken-down wooden gate in her front yard. Miss Jennings was the only person in the neighborhood who didn't care much about the appearance of her property. She didn't have time for tasks like cleaning. She was much too busy informing the neighbors of one another. Besides, the way Miss Jennings saw it, she'd done enough cleaning and tidying up as a child at the Swan Orphans Home, where she was raised.

As she put her hand on the gate handle, she looked to see if there were any lights on at Mr. Spindle's house. "Good. He's still asleep," she whispered to herself. She then quickly looked down both sides of the street and saw no one. Quietly opening her squeaky gate, she ran across the street toward the maple tree, holding her robe up just enough not to trip over it. Miss Jennings reached up to the lowest branch and snapped it off. There were at least ten leaves on the branch. She stuck it in her robe and pranced across the street with her head held up high as if everything was normal.

Suddenly, she heard a noise coming from a few houses down. Stretching out her short stubby neck, she struggled to see what it was. It was Mr. Quinch, walking his little brown Chihuahua, and to make matters worse, he was walking directly toward her. Miss Jennings quickly ran back home and quietly shut the door. She looked up at

Snowball and cried, "Can you believe Mr. Quinch from down the street is out at this hour? What kind of person is out at this time? I wonder what he's up to." Walking into the kitchen, she pulled out the branch from her robe and began to examine the leaves, looking for anything unusual, but there was nothing unusual about these leaves. They were simply green maple leaves. Holding the branch in the air, Miss Jennings shook it rapidly for a few minutes, commanding, "Fly! Fly away!" But nothing happened. "Of course it's not going to fly. Everyone knows leaves don't fly. What am I thinking?" she said to Snowball as he watched her from the kitchen entrance. She tossed the branch into her living room, where it landed on a pile of clothes that had been sitting on her chair for months now.

"I guess I'll have an early start to my day," she said as she shrugged her shoulders and held her chin in the air. "Flying leaves, hmm . . ." As the running water filled her coffeepot, she glanced out the window at the maple tree in Mr. Spindle's front yard. Sitting at the very top was a huge brown hawk; it seemed to be looking down at her.

"Oh, my!" shouted Miss Jennings and quickly closed the curtains. It was 8:30 a.m. by the time Miss Jennings stepped out onto her unpainted broken-down porch. She took a deep breath and adjusted her bright yellow-and-green autumn dress to just below her knees. The sun was shining through the huge oak tree on the sidewalk in front of her house. "What a beautiful Sunday morning," she whispered as she stepped off the first step. Although she was extremely afraid by what had happened the night before, Miss Jennings knew she had to warn the neighbors of the mysterious Mr. Spindle. She tiptoed across her front yard, trying to be as quiet as possible as she looked at Mr. Spindle's maple tree. The hawk was still sitting on the top branch. Miss Jennings held on to her broken-down fence, and with every step she took, she was afraid the hawk was going to come flying down at her.

CHAPTER 2

Another neighbor, Pam, was looking out her window as she prepared breakfast in her kitchen. She called to her husband, Paul, "Honey, hurry! You're going to miss it! There goes Miss Jennings walking down the street again in her high heels." Pam was a tall, thin woman with blonde hair and blue eyes. "I don't know why she wears high heels. She can hardly walk in them."

Every morning while preparing breakfast, Pam would look out her kitchen window and watch Miss Jennings run across her lawn toward someone's house as if she couldn't wait to share the latest news of the day. "It's like clockwork," Pam would say, if anyone asked. This morning, however, Miss Jennings was walking rather slowly. His brown eyes narrowed as he glanced toward his wife. As a laid-back kind of guy, Paul went about his own business and enjoyed sitting back on the couch on Sunday mornings, reading his newspaper. "Whose house is she going toward now?" Paul asked.

"Looks like Bella's," replied Pam.

"Good, as long as it's not ours!" exclaimed Paul.

Although Pam found Miss Jennings talked too much, she always was curious to hear what she had to say. "Hmm! I wonder why she's tiptoeing this morning. Miss Jennings looks a little frightened as well," she said softly, more to herself than to her husband.

"What, dear?" Paul asked.

"Oh, nothing," Pam replied.

That morning, on her way to Bella's house, Miss Jennings heard a little girl's voice from a distance say softly, "Miss Jennings, would you like a cup of coffee or tea?" She looked over toward the trees, and there stood six-year-old little Sally. Her mother's red spaghetti-strap dress hung loosely on her short, thin body, and the white high heels on her feet were a few sizes too big for her. She tucked her straight brown hair behind her ear, and her big hazel eyes sparkled as she stared at Miss Jennings with a smile that was missing two front teeth.

How could I say no to that face? Miss Jennings thought as the little girl walked toward her. Although Miss Jennings was anxious to tell Bella about the flying leaves, she didn't want to hurt Sally's feelings. "Of course I will. Thank you for asking."

Sally and Miss Jennings both picked up their dresses above their knees as they walked on the unsettled lawn toward the plastic picnic table and chairs that were placed in the middle of Sally's backyard.

"Beth is waiting for us," Sally said in a ladylike tone.

Miss Jennings couldn't wait to get to the picnic table. Her ankles were sore walking in high heels across the lawn. As she approached the picnic table, she reached for the nearest chair and began to sit down.

"No! Not there!" a pudgy girl with long, curly black hair yelled out angrily. The seven-year-old—Sally's friend Beth—was wearing her older sister's blue summer dress, which was too big for her. Her brown straw hat was pulled down just below her eyebrows, so that she had to tilt her head up to peer at Miss Jennings. She pointed to the next chair over. "There!" she said more calmly. "You almost sat on Sam. You must apologize!"

"Please accept my apology Sam," Miss Jennings said politely. "I did not see you there."

"This is Sabrina," Sally said to Miss Jennings with a smile, as she pointed to an empty chair. "What is your friend's name?" Beth asked Miss Jennings, pointing to a spot right next to the woman.

She had to think quickly. "Well . . . well . . . Sara. Yes, her name is Sara."

"What a lovely name. It's a pleasure to meet you, Sara," Beth said, as she picked up her teacup and took a little sip.

"She said it's a pleasure to meet you as well," Miss Jennings replied.

"We can hear!" Beth and Sally replied sternly.

"Oh . . . of course," Miss Jennings said as she sank into her chair.

"Coffee or tea?" Sally asked.

"Tea, please. No sugar or cream—I'm on a diet," Miss Jennings replied in a serious tone.

"Sam and I will have coffee, please," Beth replied.

Sally grabbed the glass teakettle off the table and slowly poured Miss Jennings her tea and then grabbed the metal coffeepot and filled four cups of coffee.

"We are planning a wedding," Beth said to Miss Jennings.

"You are, are you?" Miss Jennings replied.

"Yes, Sam and Sabrina are going to be married by the end of the month. Would you like to come?"

"Sure, I would love to come," Miss Jennings replied as she held her teacup to her mouth.

"We are going to have lots of flowers and cake," Sally said with a smile.

"It sounds lovely," Miss Jennings replied. Just as she was about to take a sip of her tea, she noticed some loose tea leaf particles floating on the top. "Oh, my!" Miss Jennings yelled.

"Don't be shy," Beth said with excitement as she helped Miss Jennings put her teacup to her mouth. Miss Jennings did not want to hurt Beth's feelings, so she drank the cold cup of tea down as quickly as possible, almost choking in between swallows. Beth and Sally sat in their chairs with their legs crossed like classy little old ladies, holding their coffee cups in one hand with their pinky finger sticking out, and continued talking about the wedding.

"Would you like to have another cup of tea?" Sally asked Miss Jennings, once Miss Jennings had placed her empty teacup on the table.

"Oh, no, thank you, girls. I must run along now," she replied quickly, trying not to gag. She quickly got up off her chair, spitting out pieces of tea leaves into her pink napkin with every step she took.

"Don't forget about the wedding at the end of the month, Miss Jennings. We'll send you an invitation!" Beth called out as Miss Jennings hurried across the lawn.

As Miss Jennings approached Bella's front door, she ran her fingers through her curly red hair to give it some bounce. She turned the doorknob and found the door was unlocked, so she let herself in, as she normally did. "Woo-hoo, Bella!" she called out as she closed the door behind her. "Bella, are you up?"

Bella stumbled out of her bedroom and whispered down the stairs. "Shhh! John's still asleep. I will be right down. Make yourself at home." She went back into her bedroom and slipped on her green silk robe, which was hanging on the end of her bedpost. Bella lived five houses down from Miss Jennings on the opposite side of the street; she'd lived there all her life. She was the only person in the neighborhood who would put up with Miss Jennings's bluntness, because Miss Jennings always had been kind to Bella, even as a child. Bella remembered many times when Miss Jennings baked her chocolate chip cookies when Bella wasn't feeling well. Even when Bella became an adult, Miss Jennings would bake cookies for her on her gray days. Bella felt bad for Miss Jennings because she did not have any friends or family.

"Let me know when she's gone," Bella's husband, John, said as he put his pillow over his head. John did not care much for Miss Jennings. He thought she was annoying and rude, but he put up with her because Bella had taken her in as part of the family years ago.

Jack, their seven-year-old son, didn't care much for Miss Jennings either. He also thought she was annoying and rude, especially when she teased him about his best friend, Arthur. The two boys did everything together—they walked to school, played cowboys and Indians, raced cars, played checkers, and swam in the nearby lake. Jack's favorite thing to do with Arthur was playing pirates, especially since he got a wooden sword. Jack thought Arthur was great; Jack loved him. Jack could say anything he wanted to say to Arthur and share his deepest secrets, and Arthur would never say a word to anyone.

Jack looked like his mother—they both were thin, with black hair and big brown eyes. Jack's twin sister, Emma, looked like her father—they both were tall, with dark brown hair and blue eyes. Lucy, their older sister, did not mind Miss Jennings's company at all. In fact, Lucy looked forward to her visits, for that was when she would get the inside information on Rob, the cutest boy on the block. Lucy had long curly brown hair and brown eyes. She would turn thirteen years old in a few weeks. She was very friendly at times, but she did not have much patience for Jack or Emma.

Miss Jennings pranced into the kitchen and pulled out a chair at the kitchen table. She made herself at home while she waited for Bella. She filed her fingernails and thought how strange Mr. Spindle had acted as the full moon had shined down on Chestnut Street. She could hear Bella walking toward the kitchen, so she placed her file back into her purse and quickly fluffed up her hair with the tips of her fingers.

"Good morning, Aunt Jennings," Bella said with a smile. She called Miss Jennings "aunt" even though they were not related. Bella entered the kitchen, dragging her black slippers across the cool tile floor as she tied her green robe together. "How are you this morning?" she asked as she gave Miss Jennings a little peck on the cheek.

"Just wonderful, dear, and you?"

"Good. Would you like a cup of coffee?"

"Of course," Miss Jennings replied. Bella began to fill the coffee pot with water. "Did you happen to see how bright the full moon was last night?" Miss Jennings asked.

"No, I didn't notice," Bella replied.

"Oh, well, I did, and it was quite bright!" Miss Jennings proceeded to tell Bella what had happened the night before.

"Flying leaves, Miss Jennings? Do you mean leaves falling off the branches from the wind?"

"No, Bella dear, I mean *flying* leaves."

CHAPTER 3

Jack and his best friend, Arthur, who had spent the night, sat at the top of the stairwell for an hour, listening to every word Miss Jennings had to say about Mr. Spindle.

"I don't think he's strange," Jack whispered to Arthur. "Do you?"

Suddenly, a large pale green button that was in the handle of Jack's wooden sword fell out and bounced noisily down the stairs. Jack tried to reach for it but couldn't quite catch it. Bella and Miss Jennings ran out of the kitchen, into the corridor, and saw Jack standing in the middle of the staircase, wearing his blue pajamas and his father's black work boots, which came up almost to his knees. He held his sword in the air as he looked down at them.

"Are you all right, honey?" Bella asked. Jack didn't answer her. He quickly ran down the stairs in between them and picked up the button off the floor. He held it tightly in the palm of his hand as he ran, fast as lightning, back upstairs to his bedroom. His bedroom was the entire attic. It had slanted ceilings with two skylights on each end. His bed sat directly beneath one of the skylights, which he liked very much, because he enjoyed watching the stars at night before falling asleep. His walls were painted light blue with dark blue borders. The wooden floor was old and stained in some areas. It creaked when he walked on some of the boards. He had plastic airplanes hanging from the ceiling and stuffed animals piled up in one corner of the room. An old iron train set Jack's grandfather Joseph had built for him ran along the entire perimeter and circled once every morning at 5:00. The plastic train conductor would pop his head out and whistle for several seconds—that was Jack's alarm clock. It had been a couple of years since Grandpa Joseph passed away, and the train set still worked like a charm.

Jack lay back on his bed, waiting for Miss Jennings to leave. He held the shiny button in the air toward the skylight and squinted his brown eyes, looking through one of the four small holes of the button. It seemed to sparkle brighter and brighter as the sun shined through it. Two black crows pecked at the skylight, trying to make their way in, but Jack paid them no mind. He didn't even hear the noise, for that matter; he was too fascinated by the sparkles on the button. The crows had been there, watching him, for months, but he hadn't noticed them, nor had he noticed the huge brown hawk that sat on the tree branch near his house. And he certainly hadn't noticed the signs that had been coming his way, such as those from Mrs. Sweeden, who lived down the street and with whom no one got along, not even Miss Jennings. In fact, Miss Jennings avoided Mrs. Sweeden at all costs. Jack thought that was unusual, because Miss Jennings would talk to a killer whale if she could.

One day, Mrs. Sweeden slipped an odd recipe under Bella's front door, a recipe that didn't make any sense whatsoever. It called for a cup of flour, a pinch of salt, and a dash of black pepper, and in big letters, the recipe's instructions read: DO NOT STIR. That's all it read. No other information was given. Ever since then, the words "flour, salt, and black pepper" kept popping up on street signs, on front pages of the newspaper, in television news, and in songs, for that matter. Bella thought it was strange, because she hadn't asked Miss Sweeden for a recipe.

Now, Jack sat up and grabbed his sword from the side of his bed. He slowly placed the button back into the slot of the handle and began to swing the sword at Arthur, saying, "Who goes there?" He hadn't parted with the sword since his mother had bought it for him several months ago from a local thrift shop.

Bella and Miss Jennings continued having the conversation about the flying leaves until Miss Jennings noticed Miss Beckett was picking weeds from her garden.

"Oh my, there is Miss Beckett," Miss Jennings said. "I haven't talked to her in ages. I wonder if she still works for that bully Mr. Peach down at the pharmacy." She quickly got up off the chair, pulled her dress down below her knees, and said, "Bella, honey, I must run." She reached over and squeezed Bella's cheeks and quickly walked out the back door.

Standing at the kitchen window, Bella watched Miss Jennings practically run across the lawn toward Miss Beckett's garden. Of course, Miss Beckett pretended not to see her and quickly gathered her garden tools, put them in her basket, and headed into her house.

"I bet she locks the door," Bella said out loud.

Miss Jennings wasn't shy. She went straight to Miss Beckett's back door and knocked. After a few minutes of waiting for Miss Beckett to answer the door, Miss Jennings noticed Mr. Donnday getting into his car across the street. So she gave up on Miss Beckett and headed toward Mr. Donnday. As usual, as soon as he noticed her coming toward him, he drove off as fast as he could. Miss Jennings suddenly stopped in her tracks and fluffed up her hair and continued to visit the other neighbors. She wasn't picky; she would talk to anyone who would listen. By the end of the evening, everyone in the neighborhood was well aware of the flying leaves.

After what seemed like hours, Jack quietly pressed his ear against the floor near the opening of the stairwell to hear if Miss Jennings was still in the kitchen. It was very quiet; all he could hear was the screeching in the distance of flying crows. As he let down the attic stairs, the smell of fried bacon took his breath away. Bacon was his favorite thing to eat. Just when he was about to take his first step, he grabbed his sword, pointed it in the air, and yelled out, "Stay where you are, you thief! I shall return." He then ran down the stairs with his sword in the air. As he reached the bottom of the staircase, Emma jumped out from behind the chair, holding out a small wooden broomstick and wearing her mother's black satin dress. She also wore Bella's white high heels, which almost fell off her feet as she jumped up. She held up the dress above her ankles with one hand as she pointed the end of the broomstick at Jack with the other, yelling, "I'll put a spell on you if you think you are going to eat my bacon."

"On guard, you witch!" Jack yelled back as he swung his sword at her. They began to swing the broom and sword at one another for several minutes. All of a sudden, the tip of Jack's sword turned into a snake's head, hissing at the broomstick. Emma didn't notice a thing; she was frantically swinging at the sword with her eyes closed, afraid she would be hit in the face. Jack stopped quickly, as he was stunned by the snake's head hissing at the broom.

"When you are going to grow up?" Lucy said as she pushed Jack out of the way from the bottom of the staircase. It was then that Emma stopped swinging, and Jack pulled his sword away from her as fast as he could. The snake's head immediately disappeared, and the sword turned back to a pointed wooden edge.

"Ouch!" Lucy said as she stepped on a white button in the corridor that led to the kitchen. She bent down and picked it up. Holding it in the air, she called out to her mother, "Someone lost a button!" She placed the button on the table, sat down in a chair, and rubbed her bare foot. Jack sat beside her and kept looking at the tip of his sword, wondering if he was seeing things. As he was chewing on a crispy piece of bacon, he looked across the table at his father, who was holding up the newspaper. On the front page, the headline read "Recipe of the Week: a cup of flour, a pinch of salt, and a dash of black pepper."

Where did I see that recipe? he questioned himself.

Emma suddenly interrupted his train of thought, asking, "Jack, do you want to try my new recipe?" She held her black witchcraft book in her hands as she gave him an evil look. Emma enjoyed pretending she was a witch. In fact, she would pretend so often that Jack actually thought she believed she was a witch. She would use Jack as her guinea pig to try her new recipes and spells from time to time. For the most part, Jack would go along with her. But at times, he was a little frightened of her evil look, especially when she would try to put a curse on him. But on that particular morning, Jack was in no mood to play witchcraft stuff. He couldn't help think, *How in the world could my sword turn into a snake?*

"No," Jack replied in a serious tone.

"Why not? You scared? It's a new drink I created. You'll like it. It's called Blue Tears! It sort of tastes like cotton candy."

"No, I'm not scared. I just don't want to!" Jack said angrily

"You look scared," Emma said.

"That's enough," Bella called out as she placed a large bowl of scrambled eggs in the middle of the table. "And Emma, what did I tell you about wearing my makeup?"

Emma looked up at her mother with bright red lipstick smeared all over her lips. "Sorry, Mom, it won't happen again." Emma placed the book on the table and filled her bowl with cereal. She didn't like scrambled eggs. Jack did. He filled his plate with scrambled eggs and bacon.

Shortly after, Jack decided to read Emma's new recipe. He was trying to take his mind off the snake episode. He slowly pulled the book toward him as he looked at Emma to be sure she wasn't watching him. Emma wasn't paying attention; she was reading the back of the cereal box. Before opening the book, he quickly glanced up to see if anyone else was watching him.

John, his father, had his head buried in the newspaper at the other end of the table. Lucy was texting on her new cell phone, and Bella was on the telephone, inviting Mr. and Mrs. Beard from next door to Lucy's thirteenth birthday party, which was going to be in a few weeks. That day, however, wasn't only going to be special for Lucy. It would be a day to remember for Jack, Emma, and Miss Jennings.

CHAPTER 4

Jack slowly opened Emma's witchcraft book to the first page. It read:

To make a flower bloom, mix a spoonful of baking powder and a dash of lemon juice. Pour it on a seed. Let sit for five minutes. Flower will bloom.

He turned to the next page.

How to make a flying carpet: Mix one teaspoon of baby powder and one teaspoon of pancake mix. Stir for one minute and slowly sprinkle onto a carpet—any carpet. Wait ten minutes. The carpet will suddenly begin to fly.

"This is silly," he muttered, but he was curious, so he continued to read. He flipped through a few pages to page thirteen.

How to make a magin appear: one cup of flour, a pinch of salt, and a dash of black pepper. Put in a plastic bowl. Do not stir. Place the bowl in the middle of the floor and step away. A magin will appear.

Jack nodded his head as he flipped through a few more pages.

How to turn pasta into snakes: Grab a handful of dry pasta. Sprinkle a little garlic salt on top, and let sit for ten seconds. Pasta will turn into snakes.

Jack giggled softly as he read the recipe about the pasta. Then he thought to himself for a moment. *Let me prove to Emma how ridiculous this book is.* He lifted the cover off a glass jar filled with dry pasta on the counter. He grabbed a small handful and placed it in the middle of the table. He then grabbed the garlic-salt shaker, which was on the shelf with all the other seasonings. Just when he was about to sprinkle a little on the pasta, he took a quick look around to be sure no one was watching him. Everyone seemed to be in the same position as they were several minutes earlier. He quickly sprinkled a little of the garlic salt. He watched the pasta closely as he sat back down in his chair. He counted to ten . . . but nothing happened.

"See . . ." he said, but then all of a sudden, he noticed a couple of the pastas move. Jack rubbed his eyes and took a closer look. Suddenly, every one of the pastas began to expand and wiggle. "Um . . . ummmm," Jack stammered. He tried to get anyone's attention, but no one paid him any mind. Moments later, there were snakes wiggling all over the table. They were white and slimy. Some moved toward his father's coffee cup and began to climb up the side. He quickly grabbed the spoon out of the scrambled egg bowl and began to whack the snakes. Dry pasta flew all over the floor.

"What in the world are you doing?" John yelled at his son, peering over the top of his newspaper.

"Yes, Jack! What are you doing?" Lucy asked.

Jack quickly looked up at Bella. "Snakes . . . snakes . . . everywhere. Look!" He pointed at the table. Bella placed the phone down for a moment. John, Bella, Lucy, and Emma looked on the table but did not see any snakes at all. All they saw was a dry pasta spread all over the place.

"I thought you didn't want to try my recipe," Emma said as she giggled and grabbed her book off the table.

"Here's a broom," Bella said sternly. "You can sweep up the mess you just made."

Sweeping the dry pasta off the floor, Jack saw a couple pieces wiggle as he swept them into the dustpan. Suddenly, he heard commotion coming from upstairs. He quickly looked at Bella; she didn't seem to notice any commotion. Then he looked at his father to see his reaction to the noise. But his father didn't seem to notice any noise either. So Jack ignored it, thinking he was hearing things. He continued to clean the mess until he heard the commotion again. It seemed to be getting louder. Still, no one seemed to hear a thing besides Jack. He quickly picked up the rest of the pasta and put the broom and dustpan away. He slowly walked up the stairs, following the ruckus. As he reached the top step, he realized the noise was coming from his bedroom up in the attic. He grabbed the dangling rope from the ceiling and slowly pulled it down, just enough to see if he could see anyone. Suddenly, the ruckus stopped, but he heard someone from the attic say.

"You can't make the journey, my lord. It's too far. You no longer have the strength."

"Can't he? I have waited a long time for this moment," another voice responded.

"He doesn't have a choice. He must return it, or he will be cursed."

"The Conway witches are aware of its presence, Arthur."

"I know, I know. With my help he will make it."

Jack still held the attic rope between his hands, but he began to shake so nervously, it slipped away, slamming the staircase against the ceiling. Suddenly, it became very quiet. Holding his sword close, he waited a few minutes before he pulled down the ceiling ladder again. He slowly climbed up and peeked into his bedroom. He looked around to see who had been talking, but he didn't see anyone.

Standing in the middle of his room, he felt a cool breeze on his back. He looked up and noticed one of the skylight windows was open.

"I didn't open the window," he whispered. He immediately pulled down on the rope that was dangling from the window and pulled on it to shut the window.

CHAPTER 5

It was a bright Saturday morning. Several weeks had passed since Jack heard strange voices coming from his bedroom and Miss Jennings saw the flying leaves. Jack was awakened on this day by Miss Jennings's squeaky voice coming from under the ceiling ladder. She was in the corridor with his sister, Lucy. Jack peeked through the floorboards at Lucy and Miss Jennings.

"Happy birthday, dear," Miss Jennings said.

"Thank you, Miss Jennings," Lucy replied.

"I wanted to be the first person to give you a gift on your special day," she said as she handed her a small white box with purple ribbon wrapped around it.

"May I open it now?" Lucy asked.

"Of course," Miss Jennings said with a smile.

Lucy slowly untied the ribbon. She opened the box, and inside was a butterfly necklace. "It's beautiful!" Lucy exclaimed. "May I?" she asked as she held it up to her neck. Miss Jennings helped her put it on. Shortly after, Jack saw them walk away and go down the stairs.

He sat up on the edge of his bed, rubbing his eyes for a few moments. Then he grabbed his blue jeans and black T-shirt off a pile of clean clothes that was on top of his bureau. He put them on and then wiggled his toes into his brown sandals. He reached for his sword and headed downstairs.

Everyone was in the backyard, preparing for Lucy's birthday party—everyone except Emma. She was on the couch, watching her favorite program. Jack was just about to go out into the backyard when he noticed Emma's recipe book on the kitchen counter, opened to the recipe that read, "How to make a magin appear," He began to read it again and thought he would try it, since he had no idea what a magin was.

To make a magin appear: Put one cup of flour in a round plastic bowl. Add a pinch of salt and a dash of black pepper. Blow into the bowl very softly and then stand back.

Jack was curious about this magin thing, so he looked over to the living room to see if Emma was still lying down watching her program. Sure enough, she was. He grabbed a small plastic bowl from the cabinet and added what the recipe called for. He looked around to be sure no one was watching, and then he slowly blew into the bowl. Suddenly, it began to snow—violet-colored snow. He quickly put the bowl down and stood up straight against the wall, with his sword held tight in his hands. At first, the snow came down like a mist, very gently. Jack held his hand out as the snow ran through his fingers.

"Wow," he whispered. Then it began to snow heavily, and it got very windy and cold. He shivered as the wind blew him into the corner of the room. The notes on the refrigerator were blown off, the white lace tablecloth flew off the table, and the curtains flopped up and down. Jack held on to the wrought-iron kitchen hutch with one hand, while holding his sword with all his strength in the other hand. After several minutes, the wind began to die down. The snow began to spread wider across the kitchen. In the distance, a narrow road began to form. Huge trees popped out of the cabinets, walls, and floor. They pushed through the roof as if it was paper. Wild grass grew off the sides of the floor. The road seemed as if it was a mile long. A brown deer came out from behind one of the trees, while beautiful large birds flew in between the tree branches, gliding gently as the sun shined on them. The blue and red colors on the tips of their wings were so vivid that Jack couldn't help but stare. Moments later, in the far distance, he noticed something coming down the road, directly toward him. He opened his eyes as wide as he could to try to see what it was. As it got closer, it got bigger and louder. Jack bent down for cover as the deer ran by him and through the wall behind him. The forest was a mile long behind him as well. At this point, Jack could hardly breathe.

"Jack!" he heard someone cry out to him. He looked over his shoulder and to his surprise, Emma was in the forest, holding on to a tree branch. Jack quickly reached out to Emma, sword in hand. His sword went through the wall, but he couldn't get his hand through.

"Help me, Jack!" Emma cried as she held out her hands.

"Grab it! Grab the sword!" he yelled at her. She quickly let go of the branch and grabbed the tip of the sword with both hands. He pulled her toward him, but he wasn't able to pull her through the wall. Suddenly, he heard a roaring noise coming from behind him. He quickly turned around to see something charging at him. He dropped to his knees and put his arms over his head for safety. A cloud of dust and snow covered him. He slowly took his arms away from his face. Directly above him stood a huge archer, holding a golden bow and arrow into the air. From the neck up, he was a white man with long, straight black hair and big blue eyes. From the neck down, he had the body of a black horse with pearl-white wings. Jack was scared; he slowly moved his sword closer to his chest as he heard a voice coming from behind the archer. Trying not to move, he stretched out his neck to see whose voice it was.

"Thanks for the ride," he heard a man say. There stood a little man with torn brown pants, the ends of which hung just above his ankles. He wore a torn button-down brown shirt with a few buttons missing. He kicked his black boots against the leg of the kitchen table, trying to get the snow off. The archer slowly turned around and pointed his bow and arrow at the tallest tree. He began to run down the dirt road. Then he spread his pure white wings out wide and flew toward the horizon, taking the forest and the snow with him. The forest began to disappear.

"Jack!" Emma called again as she slowly began to disappear with the forest.

"Emma!" he cried out as he tapped on the wall. Jack could hear the little man still kicking the leg of the table.

The little man cleared his throat and said, "Finally! It's about time you picked up on my signs. I sent you the recipe five times. I was beginning to worry about you. For a minute there, I thought the witches of Conway were going to win this battle." He wiped the snow off his long white beard.

Jack thought that the man must have been at least a hundred years old. He was short and thin, although he had a round belly. His nose was as cute as a button, and his big brown droopy eyes made him look helpless. His hair was dark brown, long, and stringy, while his beard fell over his round pot belly. "Don't be alarmed, Jack," he said as he approached. "Boy, you look much taller in person. Turn around." He twirled his finger in a circular motion.

Jack noticed the man was very hyper. Jack slowly turned in a circle, trying not to take his eyes off the little man.

"Who . . . who are you?" Jack asked.

"Heck, I'm Arthur, your magin—you know, your imaginary friend. We're called magins in our world. However, I am known by many names." With a big smile, he gave Jack a big bear hug. Jack didn't move. In fact, he could hardly breathe.

"Emma—my sister—is in the wall," Jack said, confused.

Arthur approached the wall and felt it. "That was unexpected. Don't worry; we'll get her back. What's going on out there?" he asked as he looked out the screen door.

"Don't go out there," Jack said. "It's my sister Lucy's birthday party."

"Birthday party! I love birthday parties. Don't worry. No one can see me but you," Arthur said as he stepped out onto the deck. Jack watched as Arthur walked into the crowd of people. He couldn't believe what he was seeing. In the middle of the yard danced a beautiful young woman, dressed in a long red velvet dress. Her curly black hair swung back and forth as she swayed slowly to the music. Lucy was playing in the background. Her big brown eyes sparkled as the sun shined on her face. No one seemed to notice her but Jack.

"Well, aren't you coming?" Arthur yelled out from the crowd. Jack slowly stepped out of the house and joined him.

"That's Cindy; she's a magin," Arthur said. "In fact, she's Jessica's magin."

Jessica was Jack's cousin, a nine-year-old girl with blonde curly hair that sat just above her shoulders. She was tall and thin and loved to dance. She wanted to be a dancer when she grew up, but she was a little shy. Sitting on a black wicker chair in her yellow-and-white polka dot dress, she tapped her feet on the ground very slightly, hoping no one would notice.

"That gentleman there," Arthur said, pointing toward the picnic table, "is Max. He's Peter's magin."

Peter was five years old. He was at the party with his older sister, Sue. Sue was one of Lucy's best friends. In the corner of the yard stood Mr. and Mrs. Georgia. They were bickering with one another, as they normally did.

"Don't mind them, Arthur," Jack said. "They always argue. Most people don't understand why they even are a couple."

"Have you ever heard the expression, there's something about him; I don't know what it is?" Arthur asked in a girlish tone. "Well, it's not their fault they're together. It's because their magins are in love, and their energy pulled them together. So they are drawn to each other because of this. And when magins are in love, they stay together forever. That is why it is so hard for you people to find true love."

Jack glanced at him strangely and then looked around the yard, admiring some of the magins, until he noticed a shadow coming from the trees above. He looked up, and there were storks flying in different directions, carrying newborn babies in pink and blue fleece blankets hanging from their yellow beaks. Magins sat on their backs, holding white lace, which was wrapped around their feathery necks, and guided them as they flew over rooftops.

"Gather around everyone!" Bella yelled. "We are going to sing 'Happy Birthday' to Lucy," she continued.

Everyone gathered around the picnic table and began to sing "Happy Birthday." The candles could barely stay lit with the cool breeze blowing in the air. Around Lucy flew two beautiful fairies. The lady fairy had long brown straight hair with brown eyes. She was wearing a brown silk dress that hung down to her ankles, white wings that stuck out from her back. The male had short brown hair and wore a brown cotton wrap, with white wings as well.

"Why are there fairies flying around her?" Jack asked.

"Those are her birth-sign fairies—the twins, Gemini. You all have one. They visit when it's your birthday. They deliver your birthday wish to the wishing well. The male's name is Gemi, and the female's name is Ni.

"A wishing well?" Jack asked. But Arthur didn't answer him.

Just when Lucy was about to blow out her candles, Gemi and Ni took out tiny glass flasks from their pockets and flew above the candles. As Lucy made her wish and blew out the candles, Gemi and Ni quickly gathered the smoke into the glass flasks. They then flew into the sky and disappeared.

CHAPTER 6

Miss Jennings pranced around the yard with excitement that afternoon. She was looking forward to midnight. It was going to be the night of the full moon again. This time she had a plan, but she couldn't keep her eyes off Jack. She found it strange that he was talking to himself, even more than ever.

"We don't have much time, Jack," Arthur said.

"Time for what?" Jack replied.

"You have a remarkable sword. But unfortunately, it doesn't belong to you. You must return it to Nemezia."

"Who's Nemezia?" Jack asked.

Arthur cleared his throat and said, "Mr. Spindle will explain everything. We must go. The sword must be delivered by midnight."

"You mean Mr. Spindle from down the street?" Jack asked.

"Yes, he is known as the button collector," Arthur replied excitedly as he walked toward Mr. Spindle's house.

Chestnut Street looked very different to Jack that afternoon. The leaves on the trees turned blue, red, purple, white, and yellow every so often as he walked by. The wind gave out a calming smell, like cinnamon sticks. Voices of laughing children carried on, as the breeze blew through his hair. The grass whispered sweet harmony with every step he took. Magins sat on front porches, playing games with children, while others walked the sidewalks with tiny suitcases and then entered houses. The sidewalk gently swayed from side to side, and Jack thought it seemed as if he was walking on clouds. But the most incredible thing of all was when an old lady stopped suddenly and picked up a dandelion from the side of a tree. Holding her purse in one hand and a dandelion in the other, she closed her eyes tightly for a moment and made a wish. She then opened her eyes and blew on the dandelion as hard as she could. The dandelions turned into tiny fairies and flew high into the sky.

"Wow, do dandelions really turn into fairies?" Jack asked Arthur.

"Yes, they really do. How else are the wishes to get to the well?" Arthur replied with a smile.

As Jack approached Mr. Spindle's gate, he heard Miss Jennings call to him, "Woo-hoo, Jack, dear!" Jack turned around to see her holding up her dress and practically running toward him. "Where are you going?" she asked.

"I'm . . . I'm . . ." Jack stammered.

"Welcome!" Mr. Spindle said as he held the gate open.

"Oh, my!" Miss Jennings said as she put her hand over her heart. Mr. Spindle held out his hand to Jack, and he introduced himself as the button collector.

"Button collector?" Miss Jennings chuckled, thinking to herself, *He's stranger than I thought.*

"Please come in," Mr. Spindle said as he held his hand out to Miss Jennings. At first she hesitated to touch him but then thought if she wasn't friendly, he might not let her in his house. So she put her hand in his, and he helped her up the stairs and into the house. She couldn't wait to get into his house. For months, she had been curious to see what strange things he might have in there.

Glass jars filled with buttons were scattered all over the floor and took her by surprise. She saw that she'd been right—there was no furniture except for a small round table in the middle of the living room and an old, brown leather book leaning up against the wall. The book was very big. It was as tall as the room was high. It had a picture of a bright full moon on the cover.

"Why in heavens would you have jars filled with buttons all over your house?" Miss Jennings asked.

"My name is Mr. Spindle. I'm a button collector."

"Yes, I got that, but why?" she said in a snobbish tone.

"Buttons are abandoned by children of all ages every day, all over the world. I collect them and send them back to Nemezia."

"Who's Nemezia?" she asked.

"Why, she's the woman . . ." He suddenly stopped speaking, as he was sure Miss Jennings wouldn't believe him. He scratched his head. Then he approached the large book and ran his fingers across some of the pages. "Here, furniture," he said as he pointed to the picture of a couch in the book. He waved his crooked cane at it and suddenly, a couch was flung off the page and landed against the wall near Miss. Jennings. She was stunned. With her mouth wide open, she sat down quickly, as she almost passed out.

"So you're the boy who will have the privilege of meeting Nemezia. May I please take a look at the sword?" Mr. Spindle asked. Jack handed him the sword. The pale green button on the handle of the sword began to give out a bright light.

"We don't have much time. We must get started," Mr. Spindle said as he approached the round table in the living room. He waved his cane above the table, and a globe appeared. It was as big as a beach ball. The waves of the ocean splashed as they hit the surface of the land. Water splashed out onto the floor every so often. Lights flickered on and off throughout all the states, and seagulls flew around the ocean, dipping down every so often as they reached for fish.

"Wow!" Jack said as he touched the water.

"Arthur, would you mind getting the tea started? I'm sure this lovely lady would enjoy a cup of tea about now," Mr. Spindle said.

Miss Jennings looked around but didn't see anyone else in the room but Jack and Mr. Spindle. "Excuse me, who are you talking to?" she asked, as she was very confused at this point.

"Arthur," Jack said—he forgot that only he and Mr. Spindle could see Arthur.

"Arthur? You mean your best friend, Arthur?" she asked as she let out a giggle.

"Yes, ma'am," Jack answered.

She quickly put her hand over her mouth and began to giggle hysterically.

"Don't worry, Jack, in a few minutes, she'll believe you," Arthur said as he walked into the kitchen.

"No time for nonsense. We must get you prepared for your journey," Mr. Spindle said.

When Miss Jennings was done giggling, she began to babble on about the busy day she had. After a few minutes, Mr. Spindle interrupted her by saying, "Your tea is ready."

She looked up and saw a teacup was floating in midair, coming toward her. "Oh my!" she said as she sunk into the couch.

"Go on. Drink up," Mr. Spindle said as he grabbed the teacup from the air and placed it to her mouth. She was so nervous that she drank the tea down in a matter of seconds.

"She drank it too fast. She drank it too fast, Mr. Spindle," Arthur whispered.

"Oh, no," he replied.

Suddenly, her face turned red and then green. She couldn't seem to take her eyes off the waves from the globe. She then began to sway back and forth as if she was on a boat.

"Is she going to be all right, Mr. Spindle?" Jack asked.

"Yes, I think so. I believe she is have a temporary allergic reaction to the seeing-is-believing tea. Don't worry. She'll come to in a few minutes."

Miss Jennings began to blink her eyes rapidly as she looked in Arthur's direction. Arthur was beginning to appear to her. "Um, ummmmm, ghost!" she said as she pointed to the side of Jack. She quickly got up off the couch and held her purse in the air. Just when she was about to swing it at Arthur, she fell backward onto the floor and passed out cold. Arthur and Mr. Spindle placed a pillow under her head. Jack grabbed a wet face cloth and put it on her forehead.

"She's going to be out for a while. She'll come to in time. Now, let's get you on your journey, shall we?" Mr. Spindle said as he approached the book against the wall. With his fingers flipping through pages, he stopped on a page with only a huge maple tree sitting on a field of grass. He stepped into the page and sat under the tree, looking up at the sky for a moment. Then he made a fist and put it to his mouth. He slowly blew into his fist toward the leaves above his head. The leaves began to change to different colors—blue, green, purple, red, white, and yellow. Shortly afterward, they wiggled off the branches and began to fly around the tree like a bunch of wild birds.

"Duck!" Arthur whispered, reaching for Jack's arm. Suddenly, the leaves flew out of the page and into Mr. Spindle's living room. Mr. Spindle followed.

"Settle down, settle down," he said. Jack was bent down on the floor, peering at the flying leaves. Some even flew into the globe and disappeared.

"What are they?" Jack asked.

"They are the birth-sign fairies. They are the leaves of maple trees," Arthur said.

"Settle down!" Mr. Spindle yelled once more in a stern voice at the flying leaves. The birth-sign fairies settled down all over the room. Some even sat on Miss Jennings's head as she lay there, out cold.

"Aries, you know better than that," Mr. Spindle said as he held his hand out to the fairy who was sitting on the mantel. "Come on, get down."

The fairy flew off the mantel and landed on the floor near the others. Mr. Spindle then softly tapped his cane on the floor three times and waved it in the air in a circular motion, creating a circle of a gray cloud in the middle of the living room. Within seconds, the cloud let out a puff sound. As it subsided, thirteen young fairies stood tall in the middle of the living room—the queens and kings of birth fairies.

"We don't have much time, so let me introduce you quickly," Mr. Spindle said as he walked up to Aries. "Jack, this is Aries, Taurus, and Sagittarius, known as Sag. They are the fairies who represent the south side of the equator."

Every one of the fairies wore long cloaks of different colors. The colors represented their birthstones. Aries was a handsome male with black, straight, long hair that sat just above his shoulders. His big blue eyes sparkled like the stars. His clear white cloak fell just above his ankles. He was the courageous one in the pack, as well as the smartest. Taurus was a short, husky young man with brown curly hair and brown eyes. His cloak was green. He was the sensitive one of the crowd. However, the bull in him came out unexpectedly. As for Sagittarius, he was tall and thin with brown short hair and brown eyes. His cloak was the color blue. Sag was the dreamer of the three. "Reach for the stars" was his philosophy.

"It's a pleasure to meet you," Sag said as he bowed and shook Jack's hand. He couldn't wait to start the journey. He had always dreamed about being a hero someday. Taurus also shook Jack's hand as a tear ran down his face with excitement.

"Don't mind him," Aries said as he approached Jack. "He always finds something to cry about." He held his head high, filled with pride and dignity. "This is Cancer, Leo, and Virgo. They represent the north side."

Cancer's cloak was red. It went very well with her long, curly blonde hair. Leo straightened out his pale green cloak as he approached Jack and shook his hand. He had short black hair and green eyes.

"So how are you?" he asked. "You have quite a sword there, do you know that?" Before Jack could answer, Leo said, "It's going to be quite a trip. I hope you're up for it." Jack could already tell that Leo had a tendency to talk a lot.

"Enough with the speech, Leo," Virgo said. She was a beautiful young lady, with long, straight brown hair and big green eyes. She was the problem solver in this pack. "Sorry to interrupt, but he doesn't know how to shut up. Welcome," she said with a smile as she stood looking into Jack's brown eyes. Her cloak was a deep blue color. In the background, Jack could hear Leo complaining to the others about how Virgo thought she knew everything. But she ignored him, since she thought he was rude. "See? I told you—he can't shut up," she whispered to Jack.

"He's not the only one with that problem," Capricorn said as he made his way toward Jack, holding his deep red cloak to the side. Capricorn always had to prove a point to everyone.

"What are you trying to say?" Gemi, one of the twins, asked in an upset tone. Gemini always thought someone was out to get them; they trusted no one. Gemi and Ni both were wearing pure white cloaks with black trim on the edges.

"Can we all get along? Please? Especially at this precious time," Scorpio said as he made his way from in between Gemi, Ni, and Pisces with his bright yellow cloak. Scorpio liked to take control of things.

"Here we go—the leader of the world is up. I can see an argument coming," Cancer whispered a little too loudly to Libra.

"Oh, the psychic speaks. I forgot you can see the future," Scorpio replied aggressively. Cancer quickly clung to Libra's arm as she put her head down in embarrassment.

"Let's move on," Mr. Spindle said. "Here are Libra, Pisces, and Capricorn. They represent the west."

"You can call me Cap," Capricorn said as he tapped Jack's shoulder. "Pisces, aren't you going to say hello?" Cap called out to her. Pisces was sitting in the corner of the room, daydreaming, as she normally did. She had quite the imagination and was a little lazy at times, living in her make-believe world.

"Walking a few feet might be too much work for her," Aquarius said as he giggled with his hand over his mouth. Aquarius wasn't shy. He normally spoke his mind. His cloak was purple with gold trim on the edges.

"Why do you have to be so sarcastic all the time?" Pisces asked as she approached Jack. Her long brown curly hair fell over her beautiful pale blue cloak.

"And I am Libra," Libra said as she got up off the floor and slowly walked up to Jack. Her multicolored cloak sparkled like white diamonds in the sun with every step she took. She was short and thin, with short black hair and big brown eyes. She was known as the peacemaker. She was calm, cool, and collected most of the time, but her indecisiveness sometimes drove the birth fairies crazy.

"And Gemini, Aquarius, and Scorpio represent the east. Everyone, this is Jack Webner. Yes, this is the boy with the button on the sword. I'm sure you all have heard the news. You have all been chosen to guide him through his journey. Make it a pleasant one." Mr. Spindle then took out a stopwatch from his pocket. "Fairies, you know what to do! Now go."

The fairies all twirled in one quick swish and turned into three-inch fairies with their birthstone-colored wings sticking out of their backs. They all flew into the globe in all four directions.

"Where are they going?" Jack asked.

"They are going to stop time—just until you return. You'll only be gone for an hour or so," Arthur said. They flew into every house, business, and church, and stopped time at 1:00 p.m.

An old man sitting on a park bench tapped his watch several times, as he thought his battery had died.

Mr. Spindle quietly set up a tent in the middle of the living room. "Quickly, step in and lie flat on your backs," he said as he handed Jack and Arthur a flashlight. "Turn the flashlights on and point them to the ceiling of the tent, and keep them on until you arrive at Black Stone Forest. There, you will find Emma. Oh, I almost forgot!" He pulled out a small map from his shirt pocket. It was rolled tight, like a roller, with an elastic around it. "Follow these directions, and you should be at Imaginary Land in no time. Now go." He zipped the tent shut.

Chapter 7

It got very quiet after Mr. Spindle zippered the flaps of the tent, but it didn't last long. Within seconds, it seemed to get very windy around the outside of the tent. Suddenly, the tent began to sway side to side and up and down as if they were on a roller coaster.

"Hold on tight!" Arthur yelled to Jack. They held on to the floor of the tent for dear life as they held their breath, at one point going under water. Suddenly, the tent landed on what felt like a body of rocks. They waited a few minutes to be sure the tent wasn't going to move anymore before they unzipped it. Outside the tent, drops of water dripped in the distance, like a faucet had a slow leak.

"Shhhh, don't move," Arthur whispered as he lifted up a little piece of the tent that had been torn. He peeked through it and looked around but couldn't see much. It was too dark.

"Hand me the flashlight!" he whispered. Jack quickly handed him the flashlight. Sticking it through the small tear, the flashlight suddenly turned into a torch.

"Ahhhh!" a voice carried out from under a sleeping bag. Jack quickly lifted the sleeping bag, and there was Miss Jennings, soaking wet, with black streaks running down her face from her mascara.

"Miss Jennings," he said with surprise.

"You didn't think I was going to let you go on this journey alone, now did you?" she asked Jack.

"But I wasn't going to be alone. I have Arthur and the birth-sign fairies," Jack replied.

"Arthur. Hmm," she said as she sat up and pulled down her wet dress. "And where are these so-called fairies anyway?"

"Great. This is going to be a wonderful trip," Arthur said as he looked outside the tent. With flames shooting out of the flashlight, Jack and Miss Jennings sat back as far as they could away from Arthur.

"We're in a cave," Arthur whispered as he climbed out of the tent. Miss Jennings and Jack both climbed out after him. Jack's flashlight turned into a torch as well.

"Hand me that torch," Miss Jennings demanded. "You're much too young to be holding fire. Bats! Bats, everywhere!" Miss Jennings yelled as she pointed the torch at them.

"Shhhh!" Jack said. They looked around for a moment, looking for a way out of the cave.

"There! I can see the sun poking through from in between the rock down there," Arthur said as he began to walk toward it. Miss Jennings and Jack followed him. Miss Jennings slipped on a few rocks on the way out. As they approached the entrance of the cave, fog lifted off the damp rocks as the sun began to rise.

"This must be Black Stone Forest," Arthur said as he climbed out of the cave. Tall trees covered every square inch of the forest. The sun shined through the branches up above, as huge birds flew in between them. Miss Jennings let out a loud scream and put her hands over her head as one flew down, missing her head by inches. The birds were completely white with large wings, a bony tail, and big sharp teeth.

"What are they?" Miss Jennings yelled out nervously.

"They're birds," Arthur replied as he continued to walk, dragging his torch.

"They don't look like any ordinary birds. Not any I am used to anyway," Miss Jennings said.

"That's because they're not. There Archaeopteryx birds, one of the oldest birds to ever exist," Arthur replied. "They're harmless. It's the two black crows sitting on the top branch over there"—he pointed to a few trees down—"you should be wary of, especially you, Jack. They are only here for one thing and one thing only—the sword. I have been fighting them off for months now—George and I, that is. It's exhausting." He scratched his round belly.

Holding his sword tightly, Jack looked up at the crows. They stared down deeply into his eyes as he slowly walked by.

"Stay away from the boy!" Arthur yelled up at them.

"What kind of birds are they again?" Jack asked Arthur, as he tried to get his mind off the crows.

"Archaeopteryx birds," Arthur said, as one charged down at Jack, scuffing the top of his head. He quickly ducked and watched it fly by. They continued to walk south. Shortly after, they heard loud noises coming from deep in the forest. They ran toward the noise, hiding behind trees every so often as they got closer. Miss Jennings wasn't quite behind them. She was too busy swiping her torch at the birds. Suddenly, the ground began to tremble from under their feet, and flashes of light lit the ground. They continued to walk closer to the ruckus, being very wary of their surroundings.

"Miss Jennings, come on!" Jack said, waving his hand in the air.

"Stay down," Arthur whispered as they hid behind a wide, tall tree. "Stay here," he whispered as he got up and ran from in between a few trees to hide behind a large rock. Jack and Miss Jennings squatted down behind the tree and watched him from a distance.

He slowly climbed the large rock to get a better look at what was happening on the other side. With his eyes wide open, he watched as giants threw boulders in the air at skinny old witches who were dressed in long black dresses and pointy old torn black hats. They flew above them on broomsticks. Lightning bolts shot out of the broomsticks down at them. Some giants were so big, they caught some witches with their bare hands in midair as they flew by. They wore nothing but large brown and green leaves wrapped around their waists like skirts. Some other giants wore the same but with added leaves criss-crossing their chests.

"What is taking him so long?" Miss Jennings asked Jack. She was beginning to lose her patience. Jack ignored her, hoping she wouldn't say another word. She slowly stood up and was about to take a step when a flash of lightning struck the side of her. She quickly jumped, letting out a loud scream.

"Sorry about that, Miss Jennings," Leo and Gem and Ni said, giggling from the branch above.

"We didn't have much of a choice. We need you to stay put. Magins normally do things like this. They give people signs so they can guide them in the right direction, but since your magin is not available at the moment, we did it for your own good."

"My own good? You scared the living hell out of me!" she replied angrily.

"Sometimes it's better to be frightened for the moment than to lose your life over a foolish decision. We have seen it time and time again. What a shame," Taurus said as he let out a tear.

"Whatever happened to live and learn?" Miss Jennings asked, running her fingers through her hair.

"Oh, it still exists. That's for small stuff, like eating too much spaghetti and feeling sick as a dog afterwards. Or cutting your hair too short and realizing you look like a poodle. Stuff like that is when magins step back and let you decide for yourself. Sometimes they even get a good laugh out of it. But when it comes to saving you from being harmed in any way and reminding you of how precious life is, that is when they are there the most," Ni explained in a serious tone.

"This nonsense is getting more and more ridiculous," Miss Jennings said.

"Arthur is coming back," Jack said as he pulled on Miss Jennings's dress. As Arthur was running back, a small giant ran out from behind a huge tree and began to chase him.

"Hurry!" Jack yelled at Arthur. He held out his hand to him, but just when Arthur was about to grab Jack's hand, the giant picked him up by his shirt and dangled him in the air. The giant giggled hysterically as Arthur wiggled in the air between his fingers. He then carefully put Arthur down. With his large head in front of Arthur's small face, he said, "It is me turn to hide. Come, find me." The little giant ran and hid behind a thin, tall tree. They could see his big body clearly. Of course, Arthur ran in the opposite direction, toward Jack and Miss Jennings, as fast as he could.

"Emma," Arthur gasped, trying to catch his breath. "Emma is tied to a tree. They are fighting for her. They think she is prey."

Jack quickly got up and ran from behind the tree to rescue her, but he didn't get far. The little giant had him dangling in the air from his shirt before he knew it.

"Put me down, right now!" Jack demanded. To their surprise, the giant slowly put Jack down. Suddenly, a young lady's voice came out from a top branch of a tree.

"I thought they were at it again. Those stupid giants and witches. I was at Zoe's birthday party in Sweden, when all of a sudden, out of the clear blue, it began to thunder and lightning," Virgo said angrily. "I was having a good time. What are they fighting for now?"

"Emma, my sister Emma," Jack answered.

"I can help you get the girl," the little giant said. He stood with a log in his hand. His crossed and droopy eyes made him look so helpless.

The ground began to tremble under their feet once more. Jack looked over his shoulder and saw three huge giants running toward him, holding even larger logs in the air.

"Run!" he yelled to Miss Jennings and Arthur as he ran between the trees.

"You no take me girl!" one of the giants yelled. He picked up Miss Jennings by her arm. Jack and Arthur continued to run, but they didn't get far. The other two giants had them by the shoulders and were dangling them in the air in no time. The giants carried them over their shoulders to their dungeon, which was in the middle of the forest in a small cave. There were several wrought-iron cages lined up against the wall as they entered the cave. Torches lit up each cage from stone ceiling.

"This is where they keep their prey until they're ready to feed," a crazy, dirty old woman behind a cage whispered. She tapped her long, dirty fingernails on the wrought iron. "Fresh blood. They will eat you first. You'll see . . . you'll see." She let out a loud, annoying laugh. Some cages held wild animals, while others held witches, goblins, warlocks, and sorcerers.

"Come here, my dear," one witch whispered to Jack with a squeaky voice. Miss Jennings quickly pulled Jack close to her as the giants shoved them into a cage. Several hours later, two giants walked into the cave, dragging Emma by her arms. She screamed and kicked as they approached Jack, Arthur, and Miss Jennings in the cage. They unlocked the cage and threw her in. After locking the cage again, they slowly opened the next cage over and dragged a small dinosaur out by its feet. It screamed and flapped its broken wings as the giants dragged him out of the cave.

"It's feeding time," several witches cried out. They laughed and pointed at the dinosaur.

CHAPTER 8

"Are you all right?" Jack and Miss Jennings asked Emma as they hovered over her.

"Yes, yes, I think so," she replied as she wiped the dirt off her knees.

"By the way, I'm Boo," Arthur said to Emma as he helped her off the ground.

"Boo? What do you mean, Boo? I though your name was Arthur," Jack said.

"I told you he was strange," Miss Jennings whispered to Jack.

"I'm Arthur to you, and Boo to Emma. You see, I'm her magin as well as yours. Since you are twins, you share the same magin. I'm not always proud of the names kids choose for me, you know. So she likes the name Boo. What's the big deal?" He walked over to the cage bars and began to shake them, trying to get the lock loose.

"You'll never escape," one of the sorcerers said from the cage further down. Sagittarius sat on the top of the cage with his bow and arrow, ready to fire. He watched the entrance of the cave like a hawk. His blue wings flapped rapidly, ready for attack. His brown leather sandals wrapped up his legs like a snake around his prey. He was ready for anything. Pisces stood behind Emma, shying away from all the others. With her pale blue wings, she sat in the corner of cage with Emma, strategizing a way out.

"I really don't see how we are going to make it out of here," Cancer said emotionally, flapping her red wings back and forth.

"You mean you can't see the future? That's a first," Capricorn said sarcastically. He stood outside the cage with his arms crossed.

"Have you lost your touch?" Aquarius sniped, flapping his purple wings. He stood near Capricorn and they giggled, but Cancer gave them a dirty look.

"This is not the time or place to be arguing. We should be trying to figure out a way out," Libra said.

"Oh, and I'm sure we will get far if we leave it up to you, now won't we?" Scorpio replied.

"I'm capable of making decisions. I just like to think things through first," Libra said. She wrapped her multicolored wings around her body.

"That's it! I'm going out there to get the key," Aries said. He'd run out of patience and flapped his diamond-color wings in the air, taking charge of the situation, as he normally would.

In the meantime, Gem, Ni, Leo, and Scorpio hovered in the corner of the cage, talking about the best way to escape. Combining these three birth signs together, however, was like pulling teeth without Novocain.

Sitting on the top of the cage, Sag sat and watched as they interrupted each other with every other word, thinking one plan was better than the other. They argued as each one tried to get the last word in. Leo flapped his pale green wings and got louder and louder, trying to convince the others that his plan was the best. But this was no challenge for Gem and Ni. Since they were so hyper and aggressive, they flapped their white wings just as rapidly and stood their ground, saying they had the best plan. Scorpio stayed calm, smiling every so often, as he continued to interrupt them and tried to convince them that their plans would not work. This went on until they heard a giant's footsteps coming their way. They all gathered close together, thinking they were going to be eaten next.

"It's the giant from the forest," Jack said. "Can you help us escape?" he asked him as he got closer. But the giant didn't answer him. He was skipping around in a circle outside of the cage, talking to himself. "Can you help us? Jack asked once more.

The giant stopped and looked at Jack with his droopy brown eyes and paused for a moment. He then whispered, "Sure, but we have to be very quiet." He smiled, showing his one front tooth, and looked around before slowly twisting the lock off the cage. "Follow me," he whispered as he walked toward the other end of the cave.

"Help me! Help me," a goblin whispered to the little giant from another cage. But he ignored him. Other prisoners yelled out at them as they walked by. "Take us with you!" They stretched their arms out of the cages.

The giant skipped all the way to the end of the cave, singing, "Me name is Oscar. I am a boxer." Jack, Emma, Miss Jennings, and Arthur stood very close to one another as they followed him. When they reached the end of the cave, Oscar hid behind a rock and said in a mumbling tone, "There's only one way out. It's through the cornfield behind the queen of giants." Oscar pointed at a queen sitting on a throne near the cornfield.

"How are we going to get by her?" Jack whispered.

"Follow me," the giant said. They followed him up a small hill. Behind the queen was a cornfield as wide as a football stadium. Only certain giants were allowed to enter the field and pick the crop. Oscar was not one of them, but he knew the queen's weakness. She liked to play "Mother, May I?" Oscar did just that almost every day in order to get into the cornfield and eat all he wanted without being noticed. Corn was his favorite vegetable.

The queen wore a gold crown on her head and held a spear in her hand. Her red silk cape draped down to the bottom of her bare feet. Oscar approached the queen and bowed to her, as he normally would. As he stood up, he said, "Queen, I'm here to play 'Mother, May I?' This time, I brought some prisoners."

"Prisoners?" She looked down and then said, "Let's play." She was so excited to have more players, she didn't mind the fact that they were prisoners. "Back up!" she yelled.

"How do you play 'Mother, May I?'" Jack whispered to Arthur.

"It's easy. The giant will command you to take a few steps, and before you do, you must ask for permission by saying, 'Mother, May I?' Once she responds, you are only to take the number of steps she permits. However, if she says, 'No, you may not,' you are to stay where you are until it's your turn again."

They all backed up and formed a straight line to begin playing "Mother, May I?" The queen pointed at Emma and called out in a stern voice. "You take two steps."

"Mother, may I?" Emma asked.

"Yes, you may," the queen responded. "You, take five steps."

"Mother, may I?" Arthur asked,

"Yes, you may," the queen said with a smile. "You, take three steps."

Miss Jennings took three steps.

"Go back three steps!" the queen ordered. "You didn't say 'Mother, may I?'"

Miss Jennings went back three steps.

After a half-hour of playing, Jack, Emma, and Arthur were behind the queen, standing on the edge of the cornfield. Oscar was a couple of steps away, but Miss Jennings was at least ten feet away because she didn't follow the rules.

"You, take four steps,"

"One, two, three, and four." Miss Jennings counted out loud with every step she took.

"Go back four steps. You didn't say 'Mother, may I?' Oscar, take three steps."

"Mother, may I?"

"Yes, you may."

Oscar took three steps and joined Jack, Emma, and Arthur on the cornfield. Sitting on the ground, he watched and giggled at Miss Jennings as he chewed on an ear of corn.

"Miss Jennings, pay attention!" Jack yelled out.

"You, take two steps"

"Mother, may I?" Miss Jennings asked angrily.

"Yes, you may."

Suddenly, Arthur heard a couple of giants walking toward them.

"You, take five steps."

"May I?" Miss Jennings asked once again.

"No, you may not! You didn't say 'Mother.' Go back five steps."

In the distance, a giant yelled out, "There's our prisoners!" The giants began to run up the hill, but the queen wasn't paying attention. She was enjoying sending Miss Jennings back a few steps.

"You, take six steps!" she demanded as she pointed to her.

"Mother, may I?" Miss Jennings struggled to say, looking over her shoulder and seeing the giants coming her way.

"Yes, you may."

She began to take a couple of steps and then quickly realized she'd better run. She ran as fast as she could toward Emma and Jack.

The queen giant yelled, "No running! You're cheating. Go back six steps."

"Hurry, Miss Jennings!" Jack yelled as he held out his hand to her. Miss Jennings reached out and grabbed Jack's hand, and they all ran into the tall cornfield.

"Run! Run! Don't look back!" Oscar yelled, waving good-bye to them with pieces of corn all over his mouth.

They ran until they couldn't hear the giants behind them. Once they reached a small stream, Miss Jennings collapsed to the ground.

"Did she pass out again?" Cancer asked. Arthur immediately ran to her and held her head up off the ground.

"I believe so. Are we going to go through this through the whole trip?" Capricorn asked.

"Probably," Gemi and Ni replied quickly.

"You all are so immature. What ever happened to compassion?" Taurus said softy.

"Oh, and you're so mature!" Aquarius replied. Aquarius always had something to say.

"Let's try to get along, shall we? I'm sure it's not that difficult," Libra said.

"Will do, Miss Peacemaker," Capricorn replied with an attitude.

Libra gave him a dirty look as she comforted Miss Jennings. "Look, she's coming to," Libra said.

"Are you all right?" Cancer asked as she hovered over her.

"I believe so," Miss Jennings replied as she sat up. Emma hadn't said a word throughout this ordeal. She was fascinated by Arthur and all the fairies. Cancer and Libra both helped Miss Jennings up off the ground.

"Can you walk?" Cancer asked.

Miss Jennings took a few steps. "Yes, thank you." She pulled her dirty dress down below her knees.

"Drink this," Virgo said as she filled a leaf with water.

Sitting on the ground, Authur unrolled the map Mr. Spindle had given him. He and Jack looked at it for a while but couldn't quite figure it out, since it was practically blank, except for a few lines here and there.

"What kind of a map is this?" Jack asked.

"It's a sun map. You have to hold it up to the sun in order to read it," Scorpio said with confidence. With the sun hardly peeking through the clouds, they held the map in the air, hoping they would be able to read something, but it wasn't bright enough. Libra spread her wings out as wide as possible and flew up toward the clouds. She blew into them, and they slowly separated just enough to let the sun peek through a little more. Suddenly, the map flew out of Arthur's hands and into the air. Within seconds, it turned into a globe, just like Mr. Spindle had floating in his living room. Trees popped out of it, and water flowed around in a circle.

"Wow!" Jack and Emma said. Miss Jennings didn't notice a thing. She was too busy sucking on the leaf like a baby's bottle. They approached the globe and began to look for anything that would lead them to the Golden Beach.

"Here—it's right here." Arthur pointed at a tiny white dot floating in the air, south of the globe.

"How do we get there? It's not on the globe," Emma said.

"Not sure," Arthur said, scratching his head.

"There is one way, the only way I know how, from here anyway," Leo said as he flew down from in between two tall trees. His pale green wings flapped in the air.

"No, we all know what you're thinking. We have to be practical about this," Taurus said.

"Why does everything you do have to be so practical?" Sag asked. "Take chances. Life is too short!"

"I do take chances. The difference between you and me is that I think logically before I test the waters. You, on the other hand, jump into things and deal with the consequences later. How much sense does that make?" He crossed his arms, his bright green wings flapping angrily.

"At least I can say I have an exciting life, unlike others!" Sag replied as he walked away. Taurus didn't answer him.

CHAPTER 9

   "I didn't come all this way for nothing," Leo said determinedly. "I can do this. I can get us to the Golden Beach. From there, we can take the steam train to the world of Nemezia."

"Let him try. What's the harm? As long as Jack and Emma are safe," Arthur said.

"What can possibly go wrong?" Pisces asked Virgo, as she imagined herself at the Golden Beach. All the other birth fairies agreed to let Leo guide them out of the Black Forest.

"Now, everyone form a circle and hold hands," Leo said. "We are going to play a game. It's called 'Ring around the Rosie.' I believe we all know how to play."

"This ought to be great!" Capricorn and Aquarius said at the same time. Arthur quickly reached up and grabbed the globe. It folded into a small square once he touched it. He stuck it in his pocket and joined the circle. They slowly began to walk around in a circle and sing.

"Ring around the rosies, pocket full of posies; ashes, ashes, we all fall down." But nothing happened—that was because Gemi, Ni, and Scorpio didn't fall down with the others. They thought it was a stupid idea.

"Can you please cooperate?" Aries asked. "I have a very special birthday party I have to attend tomorrow. Nancy Bliss is turning sixteen years old. It's the only age we queens and kings attend to deliver the ultimate birthday wish." He anxiously tapped his foot on the ground.

"We all have to fall at the same time!" Scorpio yelled out.

"Let's try it again," Sag said as he rolled he eyes at them. They began to go around again, this time singing louder.

"Ring around the rosies, pocket full of posies; ashes, ashes, we all fall down." This time they all dropped at exactly the same time. The ground opened up, and they all fell into the ground, falling hundreds of feet below through the dirt and rocks until they landed on a dark, hard surface.

Jack stood up and rubbed his leg. Arthur and Emma helped Miss Jennings up off the ground. The fairies were nowhere to be found. As they looked around, they noticed there was no sign of life anywhere—except for the noise of birds flapping their wings, bats hissing, dinosaurs screeching, monkeys swinging off branches, tigers and lions roaring in the distance, and snakes hissing. The noise filled the air like a wild jungle. All at once, the dark, round area under their feet began to move slightly. Arthur quickly realized they were standing on a spider shadow—not just any spider; it was a tarantula shadow.

"Don't move," Arthur whispered. He looked at the edge of the shadow for the spider's furry legs. "When I say *run*, run as fast as you can."

Just then, the spider began to wiggle as if it was trying to get them off its back.

"Run!" Arthur yelled as he stepped off the spider's back. They all ran as fast as they could, looking for somewhere to hide, but unfortunately, they were in the Jungle of Shadows Fall, where there was nothing above the ground. There were only shadows of animals, insects, and trees on the surface of the ground here. Miss Jennings's short legs couldn't keep up with the others. She screamed as she looked back and saw the shadow of the spider almost under her feet. The shadow crawled right past her and continued to chase Arthur, Jack, and Emma. At first, she thought she was out of harm's way, and then she heard a hissing sound in the distance. Squinting her eyes to get a better look, she noticed it was a shadow of a python snake, slowly making its way closer to her. She walked backwards very slowly, taking small steps, trying not to make a sound. Behind her, she could hear Jack swiping his sword at the spider and saying *en garde* every so often. But that didn't last long. Within seconds, she couldn't hear him anymore. She stopped but hesitated to look back, wondering if the spider had eaten them. At that moment, the spider shadow's furry leg creeped up on the side of her. Holding her arms close to her chest and with her eyes closed tightly, she shook like a leaf, thinking she was going to be eaten next. And then she was startled by Emma's voice.

"You can open your eyes now, Miss Jennings. The spider can't get to you if it can't see you." Miss Jennings slowly opened her eyes. Above her head was a gray umbrella that gave out a perfectly round shadow under her feet. She quickly looked around and watched the spider crawl away.

"Oh my, where are we?" Miss Jennings asked as she quickly took the umbrella from Emma's hand.

"I'm afraid we are in a dangerous place. The Jungle of shadows Falls" Arthur said, sounding frightened. "For the time being, keep the umbrellas over your heads at all times. The creatures can't get to us if we are a round shadow. They simply can't make out what it is, so they will not harm us." "Where did the umbrellas come from?" Miss Jennings asked Emma as she twirled hers over her head.

"Arthur had them in his front pocket," Emma replied. She smiled as she watched monkey shadows swing from tree to tree. Miss Jennings looked at Arthur's torn brown pants that clearly were too small on him. She couldn't imagine how four large umbrellas came out of such a tiny pocket, but she didn't put too much thought into it; she was too exhausted.

They walked the grounds of the jungle for a while, trying to find a way out and avoiding stepping on shadows of dinosaurs, snakes, elephants, and large spiders as they walked by. Suddenly, a loud screeching noise came bolting down from above. Jack looked up—charging down at him were the two black crows that had been in the Black Forest, the same two crows that had been following him for months. Jack quickly ducked under his umbrella and held on to it as tightly as he could with one hand; he held his sword with the other. The crows poked at his umbrella with their sharp feet and flapped their wings as they tried to pull the umbrella away from him. Miss Jennings screamed as she swung her umbrella at them, but they didn't give up so easily. They poked at the umbrella, leaving small holes all over it, which allowed the sunlight through. Jack fell to the ground as he struggled with the umbrella. With his back on the ground and the umbrella over his body, he slowly lost his grip, and the crows flew off with it. Arthur quickly ran to Jack to cover him with his umbrella, but it wasn't large enough for the two of them. Jack was exposed to the shadows of the wild. Within seconds, a lion ran over him, with his large fangs ready to bite. Jack held on to his sword with both hands and swung at it. The lion got even more aggressive with every swing of the sword. Suddenly, in the distance, a loud screeching noise came charging down again. It was a large white-and-brown spotted dragon. It was as big as a house. The birth fairies flew above it as it came charging at Jack. With one swipe of its beak, it swept Jack, Emma, Arthur, and Miss Jennings off their feet in no time. They held on tightly to the back of its fur as they flew in between the shadows and made their way up into the sky.

"Atta boy!" Arthur said, tapping the dragon's side with excitement. Arthur wasn't surprised to see Henry. After all, he was the dragon that had rescued princesses from castle for centuries. "Don't worry," Arthur called to the others. "This is Henry, the princesses' rescuer."

"The princesses' rescuer? There are no princesses here," Emma yelled out as the animals from Jungle of shadow's Fall screeched out at them.

"Oh yes, there's one," he replied. "You'll see soon enough."

"Where is he taking us?" Jack asked.

"The Golden Beach. The Golden Beach, my friend," Arthur replied. "And from there, we will go see Nemezia, where everything and anything is possible." Arthur smiled. "Hold your breath" was the last thing they heard Arthur say as Henry dove head first into the Atlantic Ocean. He swam very deep—so deep that Jack, Emma, and Miss Jennings wondered if they could hold their breath any longer. As he flapped his wings gently, he swam in between mountains and trees deep in the water. Emma, Jack, and Miss Jennings all took a deep breath, and they couldn't believe they could breathe. In fact, it was the freshest breath of air they had ever taken.

"Wow," Jack and Emma both said at the same time. It was as if they had entered a whole other world. Suddenly, street signs paved the bottom of the ocean—Curve Lane, Spells Avenue, and Red Street the signs read in big, bold letters. Henry took Spells Avenue and swam up toward the shore. Tropical fish swam beside them as they got closer to the shore.

In the distance were two huge mountains with roaring lion heads sticking out of them. Henry charged in between the mountains as the lions roared at them. He headed up toward the surface and flew out of the water and into the sky. He flew above several mountains and then made his way down to a beautiful tropical island with golden sand, in the middle of the Pacific Ocean. It was called the Golden Beach. He landed gently, placing his feet on the warm, golden sand and waiting patiently as they climbed off him. Arthur grabbed a dog biscuit out of his pocket and fed Henry with it. With crumbs of biscuit on his lips, Henry flapped his wings and flew far into the horizon.

"Ahhh, finally" Arthur said. He plopped himself onto the warm sand and lay on his back with his arms behind his head, enjoying the bright, warm sun on his face. "Now, we wait," he said as he closed his eyes.

"Wait for what?" Emma asked.

"The steam train, my dear. The steam train," he whispered.

"Ummm . . . ummm, I don't see a train track," Jack said, looking around. Arthur didn't answer him. With his eyes closed, he settled into the sand and fell asleep. Jack, Emma, and Miss Jennings sat on the beach, patiently waiting for the so-called steam train. Shortly after, in the distance they noticed a few butterflies flying out to the water.

"Arthur! Arthur!" Jack shook him until he woke up.

"Can't a magin get any sleep?" Arthur asked as he sat up.

"Butterflies flying—I mean, they're flying out of the water!"

"That's because the steam train is on its way," Arthur said with a smile.

"Wow, you don't see that back home. Where are they coming from?"

"The library of life. You see, when someone passes away, that person becomes a beautiful butterfly." He watched one fly above his head.

"That's ridiculous," Miss Jennings said as she ran her fingers through her hair. All of a sudden, the ocean became wavy—very wavy. White caps filled the surface.

"Get ready; the train is going to arrive shortly," Arthur said as he picked up a seashell. Jack and Emma looked around, but there was no sign of a train anywhere.

"How do you know it's coming?" Miss Jennings asked. "I don't hear anything."

Standing at the shore line, Arthur held the seashell to his ear. "By the waves—look at all the white caps. It's the steam from the train that makes the white caps on the surface of the ocean. And if you listen closely to the seashell, you can hear the conductor speaking."

At this point, Miss Jennings really thought Arthur had lost his mind. She took the seashell from him and put it to her ear.

"Arriving in thirty seconds"—a deep stern voice came out of the seashell. All of a sudden in the distance, a train popped out of the ocean and rode on the top of the water toward them. It slowed down as it got closer. The conductor blew his whistle as the train stopped at the shore line, and he called out, "All aboard!" Jack and Emma ran up to the train with their eyes wide open and slowly stepped in.

"Let's go!" Arthur said as he held his hand out to Miss Jennings. Just when she was about to grab his hand, he quickly put his hand to his shirt and caught a button that had just fallen off—a round white button. He put his head down with sadness and held the button close to his heart.

"Are you all right?" Miss Jennings asked.

He showed her the button and said, "I'm going to miss her. Molly is her name, Molly Shaw from Minnesota. She and I danced in her bedroom in the mirror for hours, almost every night for the past eight years. I taught her a few steps, you know. I'm a pretty good dancer, if I do say so myself." He cleared his throat. "Anyway, I expected this. Lately, she hasn't been dancing like we used to. It's hard to see them grow up, you know!"

"Aren't you coming?" Jack yelled at them from a window in the train.

"I'm sorry to hear that," Miss Jennings replied as she wiped a tear off his check. "We all have to grow up at some time."

Sitting at the window seat, Jack couldn't wait to get to kingdom of imagination to meet Nemezia. The golden steam train skimmed the surface of the water for miles until it reached the train station. It was quite a busy train station. Hundreds of magins sat on benches with suitcases, waiting to board.

"This is where we get off," Arthur said as the train came to a complete stop. Lines formed quickly outside the train. Suddenly, the hawk appeared out of nowhere. Sitting on a bench, it opened its wings up wide and folded them over its entire body and head. Within moments, it grew taller and wider. It was covered with a brown cloak. It slowly opened the cloak—and there stood an old man.

Chapter 10

"You must be Jack," the old man said, walking up to him. He was bald, thin, and tall.

"Yes, sir," Jack answered as he stared at the old man's long brown braided beard.

"Welcome to the kingdom of imagination. The name is George. I'm the man in the moon." He opened his arms wide and went to hug Jack. "May I?" he asked, holding out his hand to the sword.

Jack handed it to him.

"Nemezia has waited ages for this amazing piece," he said. "You are truly a hero." He looked over and noticed Miss Jennings struggling down the few steps of the train. He quickly approached her. "Oh, ma'am, let me help you," he said as she stepped from the last step. He held his hand out like a true gentleman and helped her off the step. "George is my name," he said as he cleared his throat.

"Thank you, sir. Miss Jennings," she said as she stared into his big blue eyes.

"My Lord, we made it." Arthur interrupted, shaking George's hand.

"Arthur!" George replied with a smile.

"This is Emma," Arthur said.

"And what a beautiful young lady you are," George said as he kissed the back of her hand. Her face turned red with embarrassment.

"Welcome to the kingdom of imagination," George said. Jack and Emma tried to stay close together as magins made their way in between them, boarding the train.

"Stay with me," Arthur whispered to Jack and Emma. He took Emma's hand and moved slowly through the crowd. Above the train station were huge clocks, each representing states and countries from all over the world.

"We must hurry. We don't have much time," George said anxiously as he read the clock that represented Massachusetts. It read 10:45 p.m.

Suddenly, a loud screech came from the other side of the train. Some magins began to scream and duck for cover as hundreds of black bats flew down at them. A black crow also flew down from a tree above and charged at George. He quickly put the sword in his brown cloak and held it tight. The crow began to circle George, ready to attack him, as the bats flew in between magins. Moments later, a puff of black smoke appeared in front of George. When the smoke cleared, a witch held out her broomstick to him. She was dressed in a red dress that fell just below her knees. Her red, long, curly hair stuck out at the sides of her pointy black hat, and her black leather boots covered most of her legs.

"Give us what we want!" she said, glaring at George with her beady green eyes. It was the witches from Conway. Conway was a small village in a forest behind Greenland, where witches, sorcerers, goblins, elves, and magins were brought when they refused to disobey Nemezia's rules. It was a scary dark place for the evil ones. Once someone was placed there, that person never could return to Nemezia's kingdom of imagination.

"I can't do that, Matilda. You're going to have to kill me if you truly want it."

"That won't be a problem," Matilda said, and she let out a loud, creepy laugh. Arthur, Jack, Emma, and Miss Jennings huddled behind a trash barrel with fear. Magins screamed as the bats bit at them every so often. "It doesn't have to end this way. Give us the sword, and we'll be gone."

"No!" he replied angrily as he held the sword tightly.

Suddenly, the bats surrounded George. They circled him like a tornado. Within seconds, the bats gathered together and formed a dark gray cloud around his body. When the dark cloud disappeared, the bats had turned into a witch, with one yellow tooth and beady brown eyes. She stood tall, looking down her pointy nose at them. Her dark blue dress fell just below her ankles. She stomped on the ground with her brown leather boots as she straightened her dark blue pointy hat on her head. "I'm running out of patience," she boomed in a deep voice.

Now standing in front of him were two witches, both demanding the sword. But George wasn't going to give up the sword without a fight. Suddenly, the wizards and witches ran out from the train station and began to shoot the evil witches with their wands. Lightning streaks filled the train station as if it was the Fourth of July. The witches laughed at them as their brooms created a shield around them. Magins hid behind benches with their suitcases over their heads.

"That's enough!" George yelled angrily. "Cicilla, my daughter, what are you thinking?" He asked with a stern voice, knowing he wasn't going to be able to protect her from Nemezia.

"Don't call me your daughter! I am not your daughter. You know why I'm here. Now hand me the sword!" she demanded in a deep, nasty voice.

"You and Matilda are forbidden to enter the kingdom of imagination. Even if I gave you the sword, you would not get far. The shadows of death will find you."

"Oh, did you say the shadows of death?" Matilda said, and they both began to laugh loudly.

Behind the trash barrel, Miss Jennings whispered, "Who are they?"

"Shhh!" Arthur whispered back, "I'll explain later."

"The shadows of death haven't been able to touch us in ages." Cicilla took out a little red flask from her pocket. "This, my father"—she held it to his face—"is the potion of forever life. So the shadows of death don't apply to us."

George tried to grab it from her hand, but she quickly pulled it away.

"Oh, surprised, are you? Did you really think we didn't steal this potion when we were dragged away by the knights of statues over a million moons ago? We have watched you shine in the moon with Nemezia all these years, month after month. Now it's time we shine. We will take the sword from you and rule the children of the world," Cicilla said in a deep, angry voice. She unscrewed the little red flask and began to drink it.

Sitting on top of the train, Sagittarius pointed his bow and arrow and shot at the flask. It shattered into a million pieces.

"You stupid fairy!" she said angrily, pointing her broom at him and shooting out a lightning bolt. Sag quickly ducked down. It missed his head by an inch. A witch standing on the other side of the train swished her wand at Cicilla's broom, and it caught on fire. Cicilla quickly banged her broom on the ground until the flames went out.

"Hand me that sword!" Matilda said angrily as she tried to grab it from him. George and Matilda struggled to the ground, but George held on to the sword with all his strength.

"Now!" Cicilla demanded. George refused. With his cloak wrapped around him tightly, Matilda struggled to take the sword away from him. She quickly got up off the ground, and she and Cicilla pointed their broomsticks at him one last time. He quickly covered his head with his cloak as he waited for the strike of lightning bolts. Just as flames started to come out of the tips of their broomsticks, the wizards and witches began to fire their wands at them once more, this time striking them to death. Matilda and Cicilla fought back until they realized they could not win this battle. Cicilla swished herself around and turned back into a hundred bats. The bats bit at George one more time as they tried to get the sword. But George's cloak was wrapped around his body, with the sword held tight to his chest.

Suddenly, a goblin only three feet tall, with beady brown eyes and dressed in ragged clothes, snuck up behind George and slowly placed a spider plant behind him. Ducking down as much as possible, he poured a little bit of water into the plant. The bats quickly attacked the goblin. He waved his hands in the air as he ran off. Within moments, the plant turn into a huge black spider—a large, hairy, nasty-looking spider that ate bats. The bats quickly flew off into the woods, leaving Matilda behind.

"Cicilla! Cicilla!" Matilda yelled as the spider crawled up behind her. Bat smell covered her clothing from head to toe. She quickly pointed her broomstick at it and tried to strike it, but her broomstick was cracked at the tip. Within moments, the spider sucked her in one gulp. The spider slowly crawled toward the woods, following the bats. The wizards and witches helped George up off the ground. He wiped a tear from his check as he watched the spider disappear in the distance.

"She was about to kill you," the goblin whispered to him.

"I know. I know," he whispered back.

"Are those crows—I mean, witches—his daughters?" Miss Jennings asked Arthur. Sitting on a nearby bench, Arthur told Jack, Emma, and Miss Jennings about the mysterious crows.

CHAPTER 11

"Many, many years ago," Arthur began his story, "Nemezia, the lady in the moon, was only a toddler."

"There is no lady in the moon," Emma said.

"Oh yes, there is. In fact, once you see her, you hardly notice George—I mean, the man in the moon." He smiled. "Now, where was I? Nemezia was the daughter of a poor couple who lived in an old broken-down house, just off a village called Surper. Right around the corner from here. Cicilla and Matilda were sisters of the well-known wizard—George, that is. He named himself a wizard at a very young age, because he could light up the world with a stone. I guess you could say he had magical powers. But no one seemed to believe him, until Nemezia came along. One day, Nemezia went for a walk. She watched George perform magic, pulling coins out of midair to entertain his neighbors. The neighbors would laugh and enjoy the show, but they didn't believe he had magical powers. They thought it was just a trick. Nemezia was so impressed that she got the courage to ask him how he did it.

"He was more than happy to teach her, since no one else believed in him. Not even his daughters, Matilda and Cicilla, whom he wanted to teach so desperately. At the time, Nemezia was only five years old. She picked up the coin trick quite quickly, and that's when it dawned on George that Nemezia might have magical powers herself. Through the years, Nemezia practiced magic and became quite good at it. In fact, she was so good at it, she was able to create fairies and magins. The first fairy she created were the dandelion fairies, because she couldn't help noticing people making wishes from them."

"Dandelions are little tiny fairies too?" Emma asked.

"Oh yes," Arthur replied quickly. "She created birth fairies as well. And magins, of course. In fact, she was the first magin to ever exist. One day she was sitting under a tree, reading a book. A dandelion fairy cried out above the wishing well in the center of imagination land. Nemezia quickly approached it and heard a little girl's voice cry out, 'I wish I had someone to play with.' Nemezia immediately followed the voice, and there sat a little girl with big brown eyes, dressed in a purple dress, making a sand castle but all alone, with no one to play with—even though there were lots of children around.

"She stuck dandelions on the roof of the sand castle and made the same wish over and over again. Nemezia heard her cries and flew down to sit beside her for a moment. Then she whispered in the wind, 'I'm right here. You're not alone.' The little girl quickly looked around as if she'd heard something. Nemezia immediately realized she could hear her. From that day forward, they played together every day.

"Emily was her name. She had quite the imagination. Several years later, Emily grew up and no longer played with Nemezia. That day, Nemezia left her a token of her love. Since that day, Nemezia has created thousands of magins for all the children in the world, so no children can ever feel they are alone."

"What happened next?" Emma asked anxiously.

"Well, over the years, Matilda and Cicilla became very jealous of Nemezia and began to create drinking potions to destroy magins and children's imaginations. That is why the world has turned so evil over the past century or so. George sent his daughters away, far into woods and forbade them to ever return to Nemezia's kingdon of imagination. Since then, his daughters have been looking for the sword, in order to gain power over the magins."

Suddenly, a clock above the station rang. Arthur looked up and saw it was 11:15.

"Everyone, settle down. We must go!" George yelled.

As they entered the train station, hundreds of magins lined up for their tickets as they waited to board the next train. But they didn't have to wait long; every time a clock struck, a train pulled up.

"Boarding Lunden!" the conductor said after he blew his whistle.

Some passengers sat on benches, eating sandwiches and such, while others sat in cafés, sipping cappuccinos. One young woman sat on a wooden bench, sorting out her small suitcase. First, she pulled out a witch's outfit and then a few long gowns, including a wedding gown. Next she took out an assortment of makeup, brushes and combs, and at least ten pairs of shoes, followed by a hair dryer and curling iron. Emma stared at the woman, stunned by the amount of stuff the small suitcase held. Suddenly, the woman was distracted by bubbles floating in the air, and she reached up to pop them. Two young female magins giggled as they watched her. Birth fairies accompanied the magins as they waited.

"Where are they all going?" Emma asked.

"They are going to see their friends. In your world," Arthur replied.

"Can you spare a button?" An old man sitting on the floor held out his hat and looked at Emma.

"Fred, didn't Nemezia warn you about this?" Arthur asked him.

The man played with his long silver beard for a moment before he answered. "I'm hungry," he replied softly. Arthur put his hand in his pocket and pulled out a bun and handed it to him. "Bless you, bless you," he said and put the bun to his mouth.

George, Jack, and Miss Jennings were way ahead of them at this point. Arthur and Emma walked rather quickly to catch up. As they reached the other side of the train station, Miss Jennings couldn't help but notice all the shops in the village. As they walked along, the aroma of fresh-baked bread took her breath away. Bakers walked the street wearing white baker's hats. Hundreds of magins, wizards, witches, goblins, elves, and gnomes crowded the sidewalks. Fairies of all sorts hovered over them. Small houses and shops surrounded the village like a perfect circle. A rather large stone well sat in the middle of a red brick platform, giving out a dim light. Baskets of fruits and vegetables sat on stands. Children and the elderly magins played in the middle of the street.

"There practicing how to play nice," Arthur said.

Emma noticed two old woman in long dresses playing hopscotch. She watched as they threw their buttons on the spaces of the hopscotch board.

"Number five," one said, tossing her yellow button. It slowly rolled and landed just on the inside of the square. "Yes!" she yelled out. "With my help, Cindy is going to beat Paula next time."

"Not if I can help it," the other old lady said, crossing her arms.

"You always win."

"I can't help it if I'm better than you," the second old lady replied with a smile.

"It's about sharing. You don't have to get it in every square all the time. You could make her button roll off the square if you weren't so stingy."

"Stingy? Stingy, you say? What about when Ana pockets all the chocolate candy her mother buys for the house and Matty is left with nothing? Now that's being stingy."

Emma slowly walked away as they continued to argue.

Wizards swung their wands in the air, practicing spells. Witches flew on broomsticks in the street. Some weren't so great at it—they would suddenly smash into the ground. One young witch, dressed in a long pink gown, caught Jack's eye. She noticed him looking at her so she decided to show him a few tricks. She flipped up and down and around the gnomes and goblins in the street. But she wasn't so good at it, because she'd only learned the flips several days ago. She glanced at him every so often and then unexpectedly lost her grip and slipped off her broom and fell to the ground.

Jack quickly ran to her and helped her up off the ground. "Are you all right?" he asked.

"I . . . I think so," she replied as she fixed her dress.

"That was quite impressive, you know—your flying and all."

"I'm a trainee. I'm hoping to get my first button soon."

"Oh, yeah, Arthur said something about that button stuff."

"I'm Elmira."

"Are you a witch? I mean . . . I'm Jack Webner."

"I've heard a lot about you. And yes . . . no . . . not sure yet. I'm practicing to be a witch. I hear that's the going thing most people want. Magic and stuff. Not sure if I can do it. I've been practicing for a couple of years now."

"Well, I think you did great with the flying and all," Jack said with a smile.

"Watch this," she said. She pointed her broomstick at a tree and said, "From dust to branches, from branches to ice." She repeated it twice, making her voice more stern the second time, but nothing happened.

Jack looked at her disappointed face. "Don't forget—you're still learning. If you believe in yourself, you can do anything." Jack said as he rubbed her back.

Suddenly, a little old man dressed in a red velvet cloak approached Jack from behind with a dozen long-stemmed red roses. Bending down, he whispered in Jack's ear, "Son, give her a rose." The old man pulled one out of the dozen and handed it to Jack. "Women love roses. They are the stem of our lives. You must always treat them with respect and dignity."

Jack took the rose, and the man disappeared. Jack looked around for a moment as he held the rose in his hand. His face turned red as he handed the rose to Elmira.

"Thank you," she said with a smile.

Walking by a big picture window near the entrance of a dance studio, Miss Jennings saw her reflection. She quickly put her head down, as she was embarrassed by the mud on the tip of her nose. "This is ridiculous," she whispered to herself as she licked her finger and wiped the dirt off, pretending she had an itch. Suddenly, she heard someone tap dance behind her. She quickly looked back. She was startled by a man dressed in a dark blue tuxedo, with blue suede shoes and a top hat. He tapped danced around her for a moment and then held out his hand to her, asking, "Shall we?"

"Oh my!" she said as she looked around, wondering if her nose was clean.

"Don't be shy," Arthur said.

After a moment, she got the courage to place her hand in his. Standing a foot away from each other, he tapped his blue suede shoes on the ground to a melody in the distance. She hesitated but then tapped right back. But he wasn't surprised. The rumor was that Miss Jennings was a great dancer when she was a child. They danced the swing until the heel of her shoe fell off. She sat down on the edge of the sidewalk and rubbed her feet for a few moments. Then she noticed a shoe store directly across the street.

An elf dressed in a tight green outfit helped her up and guided her into the shoe store without saying a word. Behind the counter was a short old gnome dressed in purple pants and a white button-down shirt. His black hair was short and spiked. He was sitting on an old wooden log, but quickly got up and introduced himself when he saw Miss Jennings. "Hello. My name is Ralph. How may I help you?" he asked in a girlish voice, holding his hand in the air.

"I need a pair of shoes," Miss Jennings said.

"You've come to the right place," he replied. He slowly walked and wiggled his butt from behind the counter.

Outside the shoe store sat an old man with a rather large pot of soapy water. He blew bubbles in the air and swung his wand at them every so often. He was mumbling something, but no one really knew what it was, because he didn't have any teeth and seemed to be drunk. However, when a bubble would pop in the air, a tiny fairy—so tiny, it was hard to see it—would fly high into the sky.

"What is he doing?" Emma asked.

"His name is Larry—I mean, Lawrence. Larry is short for Lawrence," Arthur said as he looked around for Lawrence's mother, ready to be corrected. "But everyone calls him Larry. His mother hates when people call him that. She is always correcting everyone. 'It's Lawrence, not Larry,' she would say. Anyway, he's one of the oldest gnomes there is. He helps Nemezia create fairies."

"He's creating a whole new species of fairies," George said. "No one really knows what kind just yet. He's been working on them for years now."

Suddenly, a boy on a ten-speed bicycle rode by and called out, "Read all about it," as he threw newspapers at the entrances of the shops, bakeries, and hair salons. Two young women, locked at the hips, hovered over the newspaper and let out a loud, excited scream. The front page headlines announced the wedding of Elizabeth Smith.

"Elizabeth Smith! Could you believe it? Time goes by too fast. I remember when she was just a child, and she loved playing house with me," one said. "What will I wear?" She looked over at a bridal boutique shop. "She is going to be the most beautiful bride ever. Let's hurry. I have to pack and help her find a wedding gown."

"Anyone hungry?" Arthur asked as he headed for Mitts Bakery. As they approached the bakery, Jack heard a magin whisper to another, "That's him—the boy with the sword." Jack looked at them and smiled. They quickly put their heads down as if they didn't want to stare.

As they entered the bakery, a little round woman dressed in a light green dress and a red-and-white striped apron approached them. "Welcome to Mitts Bakery. Help yourself to anything you wish." There were hundreds of pastries to choose from.

Magins stood tall behind the counters, waving their hands to get attention. "Try this—it's made of rosebuds," a young woman said. She had straight blonde hair and was dressed in a long pink printed dress and a white chef's hat. She handed Emma a huge rosebud muffin.

"Thank you," Emma said with a smile.

"You aren't from around here, are you?" the magin asked.

"No, I'm from Massachusetts," Emma replied.

"Ah, Massachusetts. I hope to have a friend from Massachusetts one day. You see, I'm still in the training process. Magins have to earn their buttons before they can have friends. I have two buttons, but I need at least three more before I can have a friend to encourage, guide, and protect. Besides, when my friend and I are ready to bake, I want him or her to be the best baker in the world."

Emma quickly took a bite of the muffin. She looked at the young woman with her eyes squinted from the bitterness of the muffin, and the woman stared into her eyes without saying a word. "It's . . . it's good," Emma struggled to say as she almost gagged.

She walked away and wiped the rest of the muffin out of her mouth with a napkin. Miss Jennings, on the other hand, ate almost everything she could get her hands on, even though some of the training magins' pastries tasted awful.

Walking by a window, Jack noticed a golden glow outside. A sign above a pine door across the street on a small stone building read "Melted Chocolate Shop." He walked across the street and pulled the door open. The smell of chocolate filled the air. He took a deep breath as he stepped inside the shop. There were hundreds of shelves filled with all sorts of different chocolate—white chocolate, dark chocolate, chocolate caramel, peanuts filled with chocolate, and animal-shaped chocolate. With his sword held close to him, he grabbed a button-shaped dark chocolate off the shelf and quickly put it in his mouth. It melted like butter.

As he reached for a second piece, he heard a man say, "So, you like chocolate, do ya?" A hunchbacked goblin dressed in a white lab coat stood there scratching his head.

"Yes," Jack struggled to say as he shoved the chocolate in his mouth.

"You're the boy with the sword. Come," he said as he walked toward the back of the chocolate shop.

As Jack stepped into the back room, it was like stepping into a chocolate factory. There were goblins everywhere, mixing ingredients together. Molds of all sorts of shapes and sizes hung from the ceilings.

"Here are some of my trainees. This is Will and Bill." He pointed to two goblins mixing a huge pot of white chocolate.

"Welcome," they said with a smile.

"Some of the best chocolate makers in the world come from the Melted Chocolate Shop. Don't they, Will?"

"Yes, sir," he replied. "Deborah from France makes the best chocolate turtles in the world. Hats off to her magin Grace Sherpher."

"Wow, I have never seen so much chocolate," Jack whispered.

Emma was next door at a clothing store. The big bright white sign above the door caught her eye immediately when she glanced out of the Mitts Bakery window. It read "Sophia's Witch Clothing and Shoes."

I'll only be gone for a minute, she thought as she snuck away from Miss Jennings, Arthur, and George. The wood-framed glass door creaked as she opened it. Stepping inside, the first thing she noticed was an entire wall filled with black boots. A sign above it read "One size fits all." The smell of leather filled the room. Witch dresses hung off racks, and hats hung from the ceiling. As she was looking at the boots, a beautiful woman in a long black dress said, "May I help you?" Her skin was so pure white that Emma thought the sun had never touched it.

"Yes, ma'am, those boots look too big."

The witch eyed her from top to bottom and then grabbed a pair of boots off the shelf and handed them to her.

"These are too big," Emma said.

"They will fit perfectly, once you put them on," the woman replied as she approached another customer.

Emma sat on a chair and stared at the boots for a few moments, wondering how in the world the boots would fit her. They were clearly too big. She slowly slipped her sneakers off her little feet and then put one foot in one boot and the other in the next. Sitting on the chair, she wiggled her toes freely in the big space between her toes and the tip of the boot. "Ma'am, see? These are too big." The woman couldn't hear her, so she stood up and took one step. Suddenly, the boot felt snug, even though they still looked too big. She took a few more steps and couldn't believe how comfortable they felt.

"How will I pay for these?" she whispered.

"They're free," Cancer and Aquarius said as they sat on the top shelf, looking down at her.

"Free?" Emma asked.

"Yes, magins make everything there is to provide their friends with whatever they need. Most of the magins in the shops are trainees—they must earn their way to becoming someone's best friend. Trust, love, honesty, loyalty, and patience, and of course sharing are the basic rules they must follow—also encouragement, guidance, and protection," Scorpio said as he flew in from an open window.

Dragging her boots on the floor, Emma grabbed a black cap and black hat and walked out of the store.

"You had me worried sick," Miss Jennings said as she saw Emma coming out of the store.

They visited most of the shops in the village. Miss Jennings got her hair done, while Jack got a new pirate outfit.

A magin sat near a dry well, catching balloons as they rose.

"What is he doing?" Emma asked George.

"He's gathering balloons. We must be short again," George replied as he nodded his head.

"From a well?" Emma asked.

"Yes, you see, we celebrate birthdays here as well, and sometimes when we do not have enough balloons, due to the trainees not making enough—that's another story—the well creates a slight suction that pulls the balloons from your world up to the well. Sometimes, unfortunately, the balloons are taken from children. We don't mean to take them, but we cannot always control the suction."

As they reached the end of the village, they saw an old stone building. It took up most of the block. Stone statues of armor stood tall on both sides of the concrete walkway, which led to the entrance of the library.

"Welcome to the library of life," George said with excitement as he held his arms out wide. The statues of armor suddenly moved and created an archway with their swords, as George led the way down the walkway toward the entrance.

"Enter, son," George said to Jack. With his hand on the rusty doorknob, he held his sword close. As he pushed open the door, his sword turned into steel and the pale green button began to glow. Holding the sword tight, Jack walked in. George, Arthur, Emma, and Miss Jennings followed. The sun shined in through the open roof. Millions of books sat on shelves. Some were very small and thin, while others were big and thick. There were twelve levels of balconies with wall-to-wall books, all in alphabetical order. Hundreds of beautiful, colorful butterflies flew out of the open rooftop from time to time. Some books were open to the last page and floated in midair, but most books were closed tightly, with different colored butterfly wings just about sticking out of them. Every now and then, a book would float out of its slot and a butterfly would struggle as it spread its wings, opening the book. As the book opened, the butterfly would fly out toward the rooftop, and the book would stay afloat in midair. A gold trimmed glass table stood in the middle of the library, with a rather thick book on it. In fact, it was the largest book in there.

"Why are there butterflies in the books?" Jack asked.

"Well, that's a story for another time," George answered.

"Yes, another time," Arthur replied.

Miss Jennings looked for her own book as she admired the butterfly wings sticking out of all the books. But she couldn't find it.

"Life is a mystery, my dear. You must take it as it comes and enjoy the flavors that come your way. Sometimes, it will be a bit bitter; sometimes it can be quite charming. Either way, it's your road to take. Listen to the whispers in the wind, and let them lead you when you are not sure," George whispered to Miss Jennings as he rubbed his fingers on a few books.

Suddenly, a bright round light shined in from the open rooftop. Children quickly gathered outside surrounding the library. They peeked in through some of the missing stones in the wall. Their laughter filled the room. Jack and Emma flinched as the butterflies flew in between them. George and Arthur bowed to the bright light as it landed on the wooden floor. Within a few seconds, the light dimmed and a white cloud puffed out from it. As the air cleared, a beautiful young woman appeared, dressed in a bright white gown with diamond sparkles all over it. She stood tall, with her brown hair tied up in a bun. She smiled at Miss Jennings as she slowly made her way to the round glass table.

George quickly approached her, kissing the back of her hand gently, out of respect. "My lady, your button has arrived," he said with pride. Arthur approached her and kissed her hand as well.

She walked up to Jack and held out her hand. Without saying a word, he handed the sword to her. "You're a brave young boy," she said with a smile.

"Thank you," he replied as he stared into her big brown eyes.

"And you, my little witch," she called Emma. "You need to practice a little harder on those spells." She softly touched Emma's face, and Emma put her head down, embarrassed. The young woman then walked to Miss Jennings and said, "Emily, it's been a long time. You don't remember me, do you?"

Miss Jennings held her head high and pulled her dress down just so. She asked in a snobby way, "Should I?"

Nemezia smiled. "You haven't changed a bit, now have you?" She chuckled and led Miss Jennings to the glass table, where a large book lay. On the cover were the words "Emily Jennings."

"Is that my book?" Miss Jennings asked.

Nemezia slowly popped the green button out of the sword and placed it in the small round opening on the cover of the book. She then picked up the book and held it up toward the open rooftop. She closed her eyes for a moment. Within seconds, the book floated out of her hands and began to twirl in the air. It wasn't long before the book turned into a crystal ball. It was as large as a beach ball. Laughter of children creeped out of it. As Miss Jennings, Emma, and Jack approached the crystal ball, they saw Miss Jennings at the age of five, pretending to be a schoolteacher. She had a few stuffed animals lined up, with books sitting in front of them. Moments later, the picture changed—she was the age of six, playing as a hairdresser. She dried and curled her dolls' hair. Again it changed, this time to the age of seven. She was playing dress-up and pretending she was a princess, hoping to be rescued by Prince Charming. She stood in front of a mirror, wearing a long white sheet over her like a gown. She stood on tiptoe in her white slippers, pretending she was four inches taller. She slowly put on dark red lipstick, which made her lips look much larger than they really were. Her light blue eye shadow brought out her brown eyes. She stared into the mirror with her cut-out white paper crown on her head, pretending she was trapped in an old stone castle. She looked deep into the mirror, imagining a prince riding in on a white horse, far into the distance. Through the years, she waited patiently, but unfortunately, she was never adopted.

Suddenly, a few years went by, and the next picture was Miss Jennings, sitting on a beach, building a sandcastle—all alone, as usual. While the other children played in the water, she held a dandelion in her hand, making the same wish over and over again: "I wish I had someone to play with."

"Oh, my!" Miss Jennings said as she held her hand to her mouth, remembering that very special day. "I remember. I remember." A tear ran down her cheek.

As they continued to stare into the ball, Nemezia appeared to Miss Jennings. She was sitting on the other side of sandcastle, and they played together for hours. From that day forward, they appeared everywhere together—in the kitchen baking cookies, finger painting, playing hopscotch and cards. Suddenly, the globe turned to another picture. Miss Jennings was eleven years old. As she sat on the edge of her bed, a little boy named Anthony approached her bedroom door. He held a suitcase in his hand and said, "I'm leaving in a little while. I was adopted yesterday."

"Congratulations," Miss Jennings said with a slight smile. As she watched the boy walk away, she realized she was never going to be adopted, especially since she was going to turn twelve soon.

The dinner bell rang loudly. She got up and sadly began to walk out of her bedroom. Just as she stepped out, she noticed a shiny green button on the floor near her door. She picked it up and looked at it for a moment before placing it on her bureau. The button was never seen again.

The globe suddenly began to twirl and slowly turned back into a book. Nemezia grabbed it from the air and placed it back down on the glass table, with her fingers slightly touching the button. She looked up at Miss Jennings and said, "I left you this button as a token of my love. No one really grows up, now do they? The child in you lives forever. Through the years, you only learn to behave according to your age. It's because of you. Your incredible imagination encouraged me to create magins for all the children all over the world." Nemezia smiled at Miss Jennings.

"Why did you leave me?" Miss Jennings asked

"I didn't leave you. I was always there. I'm the whisper you hear in the wind. The shadow on the ground. The smell of a wonderful memory and the courage you feel when you are scared. I have spoken to you through songs and words you've read, and I shine down on you every month. I'm the woman in the moon."

Suddenly, Mr. Spindle walked through the door, dressed in his black tuxedo and funny-looking different-colored button tie. Everyone began to clap as he bowed to Nemezia.

"We can never have enough button collectors," Mr. Spindle said to Emily as he approached her.

"Me, a button collector?" she asked.

"Yes, it is going to take many years before everyone begins to save their magins' buttons."

"Nemezia, the kids must be getting back," Arthur requested. George handed Jack his wooden sword with the empty hole on the handle. Shaking his hand good-bye, he wished him a wonderful life.

"Gather together and hold hands," he requested as he kissed the back of Miss Jennings's hand and then kissed Emma on the forehead.

Nemezia turned back into a small round light and slowly floated out of the rooftop.

"Close your eyes tightly and imagine yourself at Lucy's birthday party. You must concentrate," George said in a stern voice.

They held hands. With their eyes closed tightly, it's wasn't hard for Miss Jennings to imagine herself at Lucy's birthday party. She couldn't wait to get her hands on a grilled hot dog—she was hungry all the time. Emma imagined herself there by seeing the maple trees full of birth fairies. And for Jack, he couldn't wait to get back home to play pirates with Arthur again. Suddenly, they were startled by Bella's voice.

"What in the world are you doing?" she asked as she stood in front of them with a cup of lemonade in her hand. They quickly opened their eyes and looked around the yard with excitement.

"Boy, those hamburgers sure smell good," Arthur said as he walked from behind them into the crowd, rubbing his hands together.

That evening, as Miss Jennings was walking home, she heard Beth call out her name. "You're missing the wedding!" Beth said. Miss Jennings quickly approached and sat on one of the chairs the little girls had lined up. Beth and Sally had two large stuffed animals sitting side by side in front of a vase of flowers. They were representing Sam and Sabrina, their magins. Dressed in a white robe, Beth had pretended to be a priest and had performed the ceremony.

Although Miss Jennings enjoyed how creative Beth and Sally were, she couldn't help but laugh at Beth's magin, Sabrina, when she said, "Thank goodness this isn't real. I can't imagine living the rest of my life with you."

The first button in Miss Jennings's jar was Lucy's white button. Within a few months, her first jar was full of abandoned buttons.

Ten years passed, and Emma got her driver's license. Sitting in the driver's seat, she put her hand in her pocket and pulled out a string with her magin's button hanging on the end. She slowly wrapped the string around her rearview mirror. Turning on the radio, she smiled as she drove off, singing along with the words to a country song, "I won't forget you, baby . . ."